Mr. and Mrs. Gerald R. Swanson
Box 335
Silverton, Colorado 81433

Mr. and Mrs. Gerald R. Swanson
Box 335
Silverton, Colorado 81433

The Happy Hollisters
and the Castle Rock Mystery

The Happy Hollisters and the Castle Rock Mystery

BY JERRY WEST

Illustrated by Helen S. Hamilton

DOUBLEDAY & COMPANY, INC.
GARDEN CITY, NEW YORK

Contents

The Happy Hollisters
and the Castle Rock Mystery

CHAPTER 1

The Orange Parachute

"Look at the parachute!" shouted Holly Hollister, pointing at the sky. "It's going to land right on top of us!"

The shrill cry of the six-year-old girl standing on the lawn acted like a fire alarm. From inside the rambling house came the scuffling of feet and cries of "Where?" "I want to see it!"

First out the front door was Ricky, seven years old, red-haired and full of ginger. He was followed pell-mell by Pete, a handsome lad of twelve with a crew cut.

As the boys clattered down the steps they were followed by two girls. Pam, who was ten, held little Sue by the hand, and the four-year-old raced toward Holly as fast as her chubby legs would go.

"I can't see any parachute," Ricky said, shading his eyes.

"It went behind that big, fluffy cloud," Holly replied, excitedly twisting one of her pigtails.

"There it is now!" Pam exclaimed. "It's orange-colored."

"There's not even a man hanging on it," said Sue. "Oh dear, maybe he fell off."

1

"Something's dangling underneath," Pete observed. "Crickets! It looks like a box."

The parachute swayed in the breeze, coming lower and lower over the houses on the outskirts of Shoreham. For a moment it seemed as if the wind might carry it into Pine Lake, on the shore of which the Hollister home was situated. But another puff straightened its course.

Suddenly the children were startled by the shouts of another boy, racing his bicycle into the driveway.

"Ugh! Joey Brill," Ricky said, as the husky rider flung his bike to one side and ran beneath the billowing orange-colored chute. Like Pete, Joey was twelve, but unlike the Hollister boy he wore a frown on his face and seemed to take pleasure in annoying others.

"It's mine! I saw it first!" Joey cried out greedily as he reached for the prize.

But while Joey shouted his claim, Pete leaped up and grabbed the parachute before it could touch the ground. As he wrapped his arms around the dangling white box Joey gripped the top of the chute.

"Give it to me!" the bully protested.

"Let go!" exclaimed Pete. "Can't you see it's only made of paper? You'll tear it."

"It's not yours," Joey said hotly.

"Nor yours either," Pam retorted.

Pete examined the box which dangled from the white cords of the parachute. Sticking out of the

"Give it to me!" the bully protested.

bottom was a tube made of plastic and rounded on the end. As Pete looked at the odd contraption, Pam saw some printing on one side of the white box. In black letters was a notice which read:

PLEASE RETURN TO
THE U. S. WEATHER BUREAU

"See, it belongs to the government," Pam said.

"It must be an instrument packet," was Pete's guess as he looked at the white box.

Glowering, Joey grabbed at the tube and jerked it loose. Pam gasped. Inside were tiny batteries, colored wires and a glass tube.

"It's a radio," Pete said.

"But Joey broke it!" said Ricky.

"Who cares? The government's got plenty of money," Joey retorted. He added roughly, "I want this. I'm going to make my own radio out of it."

"You'll do nothing of the sort," Pete declared and wrested the tube away from Joey. "We'll mail this back just as the U. S. Weather Bureau wants us to do."

Pete's firmness discouraged the bully, who looked from one child to another.

"You're a bunch of sissies!" he said, with his mouth turned down, and scuffed away. "I still say that parachute's mine, and I'll get it, too." He jumped on his bicycle and disappeared down the street. As he did, another boy of the same age ran into the yard.

4

"Hi, Dave!" Pete greeted the good-looking lad. "Look what we've found!"

Dave Mead, who lived down the street, was goggle-eyed to see the package of instruments. "I'll bet it came from a weather balloon," he said. "Golly, that's great! Do you suppose you get to keep the parachute?"

"Maybe," Pete replied. "We'll ask Dad when he comes home for lunch."

The youngsters had studied their find for only a few minutes when Mr. Hollister turned into the driveway in his station wagon. The children's father was a tall, athletic-looking man with wavy brown hair and smiling eyes. As he stepped out of the car, they ran up with their treasure.

"I've heard about these instrument parachutes," Mr. Hollister said as he turned the box over in his hands. "But I confess I don't know much about them." He suggested that Pete take the treasure to Mr. Kent, who wrote a weather column for the Shoreham *Eagle*.

"And I'm certain you can keep the parachute just so long as you return the instrument," Mr. Hollister added. Pete pulled out his pocketknife and cut the box from the chute.

"Yikes!" Ricky cried out. "We can have some fun with this!" He grabbed the lines of the parachute and raced around the lawn with the orange paper flying behind him.

Just then Mrs. Hollister appeared in the doorway.

She was a slender, attractive woman with light hair and a cheery smile. After greeting her husband, she invited Dave to have lunch with them.

The Hollisters' home was a friendly place, where neighborhood children were welcome. There was always fun of some kind, or a mystery to be solved. Besides, the family's pets interested the Hollisters' playmates. There was Zip, the beautiful collie dog, and White Nose, the cat, with her five kittens. The largest pet of all lived in the garage. He was Domingo, a burro on whose back the youngsters often rode.

When luncheon was over, Pete said, "If you'll excuse us, Dave and I will go to see Mr. Kent."

"Before you do, Pete," his father said, "I wonder whether you and Pam would work for me at The Trading Post tonight."

The Trading Post was a combination hardware store, sporting goods and toy shop run by Mr. Hollister in downtown Shoreham. Like the other shops, it was open late on Thursdays.

"We'll be glad to, Daddy," Pam said.

"Me too," her brother replied.

Dave thanked Mrs. Hollister for her hospitality, and the two boys hastened off, with Pete carrying the white box in his arms.

Arriving at the newspaper office, Pete and Dave knocked on a door bearing Mr. Kent's name.

"Come in," called the editor.

The companions entered an office decorated with

6

stuffed birds and small animals, because Mr. Kent was also the newspaper's wildlife editor.

Behind a typewriter desk sat a sun-tanned man, who swiveled around to greet his visitors.

"Hello, boys," he said. "Say! What have you got there?"

"It dropped out of the sky," Pete said as he put the box in the editor's hands.

"Well, I'll be a ring-tailed raccoon!" Mr. Kent said. "This is from a weather balloon. I haven't seen one of these since I was in the military service."

"Crickets!" Pete exclaimed. "Then you know all about it!"

"A thing or two," Mr. Kent said with a wide grin. "Here, let me show you." He tugged at one side of the box and it snapped open. Inside were the wires and springs of delicate instruments.

"These record altitude, air pressure and temperature," Mr. Kent said. "The information is relayed to the ground by this radio." He tapped the tube on the bottom of the box. "When the balloon rises many thousands of feet, the pressure inside it becomes greater than the pressure outside, and it bursts."

"Is that when the parachute is released?" Pete asked.

"Exactly, and the Weather Bureau tries to salvage as many instrument packets as possible."

"That's keen!" Dave said.

The man paused and looked squarely at the two boys. "I think I'll let you in on a secret," he said.

"What is it, Mr. Kent?" Pete asked eagerly.

The editor pulled up chairs for the two boys, and when they had been seated he went on, "Something mysterious has been going on around Pine Lake at night. A UFO has been seen in the sky. You know what that is?"

"Yes," said Pete. "That's short for Unidentified Flying Object." His eyes sparkled with excitement.

"What did the UFO look like?" Dave asked.

"Strange lights," Mr. Kent said, "come drifting down from the sky, glowing blue, then green, and purple. Nobody knows what they are. The latest ones were seen by a pilot named Jet Hawks."

"Crickets! What a mystery!" Pete exclaimed. "I'd like to solve it."

"Suppose you boys act as junior reporters for me —and sleuths, too," the editor suggested.

"That would be great!" Dave declared. "We'll start right away."

"May I have the address of Jet Hawks?" Pete requested. "I'd like to ask him some questions."

The man jotted down the pilot's name and address. Pete glanced at the paper and said, "Oh, that must be the family that just moved down the street from Joey Brill."

"Yes, they're new in Shoreham," the editor said. "Mr. Hawks flies an executive jet plane for an insurance company here in town."

"I'd like to meet a real jet pilot," Dave remarked.

Mr. Kent smiled. "Let's see what you can do with this assignment, boys," he said, shaking hands with them. "And don't forget to return the packet to the Weather Bureau."

"We won't!" Pete promised as they left the office and hurried toward home.

As they came to the Hollisters' house, Pete stopped short and chuckled. "Dave, look at Ricky!" The redhead was standing on the roof of the garage, holding the orange parachute. One end had been weighted with a small lead soldier.

"Here it comes," Ricky called to Holly who was standing on the ground.

The boy tossed the chute high into the air. The orange paper umbrella opened and drifted toward the pigtailed girl. But just as it touched the ground, Joey Brill sprang from behind a bush and snatched the parachute.

"Stop!" Holly cried as Joey dashed off. "Give it back!"

CHAPTER 2

A Thunder Egg

JOEY rolled up the parachute, stuck it inside his shirt, leaped on his bicycle, and sped off. Pete and Dave could not catch him.

"That was a clean getaway," Pete said, snapping his fingers in disappointment.

By this time Ricky had climbed down from the roof of the garage. "Yikes, if I ever get hold of that Joey Brill!" he said, his chin quivering with anger.

"Don't worry about it," Pam said, and put an arm around his shoulder. "Maybe you can get another."

"But that one was a dandy—an official Weather Bureau parachute!" Ricky thrust his hands deep in his pockets and strode toward the Hollisters' dock on the lake shore.

"I wish we could do something for him," Pam said. "I wonder—"

"What?" Pete asked.

"Oh, just an idea—for girls. Come with me, Holly," she said and the two skipped toward the house.

Pete turned to Dave and said, "Let's go see Jet

Hawks now." Dave agreed and the two hurried from the yard.

A short time later they stood on the porch of a white house with a red door. Dave rang the bell and a tall, pleasant woman answered.

Pete asked for the pilot. "I'm sorry," Mrs. Hawks told them, "but my husband won't be home until day after tomorrow." Disappointed, the boys thanked her and left. They spent the rest of the afternoon quietly looking for Joey Brill, but with no luck.

After supper that evening Mr. Hollister rose from the table and asked, "Are my salesmen ready?" Pete and Pam both said yes, then hurried to the car and drove to The Trading Post with their father.

As they entered Mr. Hollister's bright modern store, they were greeted by Indy Roades, who stepped from behind one of the long counters.

"Hi, Indy," Pam said.

"How's business?" Pete asked.

"Very good," replied the short, dark-haired man, his eyes crinkling in a cheerful smile. Indy was a real Indian who had lived in New Mexico before moving to Shoreham. He was Mr. Hollister's chief helper in the store.

"Where shall we work?" Pete asked.

"Garden supplies," Indy said. "They've been selling very well."

Pete and Pam walked over to a long table filled

11

with garden tools, plant food, seed packets and little plastic bags of colored stones.

"What are these?" Pam asked, picking up one of the sacks.

"Polished stones," Indy said. "People use them to decorate window gardens."

Soon afterward customers began coming into the store. Many of them stopped at Pete and Pam's department. A young woman carrying a baby picked up one of the bags of stones. "Oh, how interesting," she said, "I'll take one of these, Miss."

But as she handed the sack to Pam, the baby knocked it to the floor. The bag burst open and the stones scattered in all directions.

"Oh dear, I'm so sorry," the woman said.

"I'll take care of it," Pete said, smiling. "My sister will give you another bag."

Pete got down on his hands and knees to pick up the fallen merchandise. The customer had left the store by the time he rose, his cupped hands full of shiny bits.

"There's a very pretty one," Pam said, as she picked up one of the stones between her fingers. It was white with tiny golden lines running through it.

"Crickets, that looks like gold!" Pete exclaimed. "I wonder where Dad got these."

The children beckoned to their father, and he came over to answer their question. "I must confess I don't know what kind of stone this is," Mr. Hol-

"That looks like gold," said Pete.

lister said. "I buy them from an old man in town named Mr. Kinder. He's a rock hound—collects minerals as his hobby."

"Let's go see him tomorrow," Pam suggested. "Maybe the stone is valuable and got into the bag by mistake."

"Good," Pete agreed. "We can mail the weather balloon instruments on the way."

Next morning Pete and Pam rose early, wrapped the instrument packet, and rode their bicycles to the post office. There, a clerk said that no charge would be made for returning government property.

Mr. Kinder's home was only a few blocks away on the first floor of a small two-family house. After reading his name over the bell, the children pushed it. A musical tinkling came from within the dim interior. Presently a small, gray-haired man appeared at the screen door. He wore gold-rimmed spectacles and had a white bristly mustache which reminded Pam of the kitchen brush with which her mother scrubbed potatoes. The little man had a serious expression, and as he spoke he constantly brought his lips together as if he were tasting something.

"Yes?" he inquired, looking at the children over the top of his spectacles. "Are you selling something?"

Pete chuckled and said no. Then he introduced himself and Pam.

"Oh, Mr. Hollister's children. Come right in," the man invited, pushing open the screen door. "Are you bringing an order for some more stones?"

"We want to ask a question," Pete said as he glanced around the living room. There were several chairs and an old television set and along one wall were glass-fronted cases filled with odd-looking, colorful chunks of rock.

Atop one of the cases sat the largest cat Pete and Pam had ever seen. It was yellow with a massive head and sharp, pointed ears. The cat's long tail twitched back and forth as the animal eyed the Hollisters.

"Oh, don't be afraid," Mr. Kinder said as he noticed Pam's startled look. "That's Casey. Toughest tomcat in these parts."

Casey sprang down, minced along the floor, and rubbed the long length of his body along Pete's leg. All the while the animal made the loudest purring noise the children had ever heard.

"Crickets, that *is* some cat!" Pete exclaimed.

"More than a match for most dogs," Mr. Kinder replied. He added, "When I go away on long trips ol' Casey comes along. He's my buddy."

Mr. Kinder made a chewing motion with his mouth and his bristly mustache twitched. "Now then," he said, "what question did you children come to ask?"

Pete produced the stone and told Mr. Kinder it had come from one of the plastic bags. "Can you tell us what it is?" he asked.

"Oh, that's titanium," the man said, bouncing it

15

up and down in his rough, calloused hand. "Now, let's see. I may have picked that up out West. I'm pretty sure that didn't come from my quarry."

"Quarry?" Pam asked with wide eyes. "Do you have a quarry, Mr. Kinder?"

"Oh yes," came the reply. "It's called Castle Rock. Haven't you heard of it?"

"No," Pete replied. "Where is it?"

Mr. Kinder said his quarry was located on the opposite side of Pine Lake. "My father owned it," he continued, "and left it to me. But the old place is worked out. There's a pond with lots of fish in it, too. I planted them myself. People use it for fishing and picnics now, but not often. It's too hard to get there."

"May we go see it someday?" Pam asked.

"Any time you like," he replied. "Are you pebble pups?"

Pam smiled. "Those are junior rock hounds, I know," she said, "but we haven't tried that hobby yet."

"The earth is full of treasures, children!" Mr. Kinder declared, and pointed to the glass cases. Big, spikey yellow crystals, smooth blue stones, sparkling purple chunks, shining silver cubes, thin iridescent sheets and many other strange, colored pieces lay side by side.

"The yellow's sulphur, blue's copper, purple's amethyst, that silver's iron pyrites, and the thin stuff's mica," Mr. Kinder reeled off happily. "Yes sir! The earth is full of valuable minerals! Not just gold and silver!

"Now your stone," he said briskly, holding it up and examining it closely. "I'll bet you thought those threads were made of gold and figured you'd all get rich."

Pete could not suppress a sheepish grin when he admitted Mr. Kinder was right.

"Oh dear," Pam said, "then that pretty stone is of no use at all."

"Oh, yes it is," Mr. Kinder said, as Casey the cat leaped up and sat on his left shoulder. "Titanium is valuable. It's used for making paint and skywriters use it."

"For painting the sky, I guess, eh?" Pete asked.

Mr. Kinder chuckled. "Yes, you could say so. It's used to make the white smoke," he explained.

With a loud meow Casey jumped to the floor, pushed the screen door open, and went outside.

"Maybe he doesn't like my jokes," Pete said wryly.

"Please tell us more about your quarry," Pam said.

Mr. Kinder revealed that it contained mainly traprock. "That's what they use for building roads," he said. "But Castle Rock was worked out long ago. Recently I had an offer to sell the place," he said, "at a very low price."

"Are you going to part with it?" Pete asked.

"No, not yet," came the reply. "Old Castle Rock is like my second home." Then with a quick movement of his head he said, "Would you like to see a thunder egg?"

"A what egg?" Pete asked, looking surprised.

"A thunder egg—that's the Indian name. Come, look here." Mr. Kinder walked to one of the display cases, opened the glass door, and took out a small, gray, rough-textured oval stone.

"It does look like an egg," Pam said.

"But instead of a chick inside of it," Mr. Kinder went on, "it has a big surprise for you children."

"How can we open it?" Pam asked.

"I'll slice it for you," Mr. Kinder said as he went into the back room. In a moment he returned with a small saw and deftly cut through the stone. As it fell into two solid parts, the children stared in amazement at the beautiful swirls and streaks of color inside it.

"Why, it looks like a scene!" Pam exclaimed. "You can see waves on the seashore and rock cliffs and sky—"

Pete picked up the other half. "It doesn't take much imagination to see mountains on this piece."

"Where did you get it?" Pam asked.

"In the state of Washington, on one of my rock-hunting expeditions. The stuff inside is called picture agate," Mr. Kinder told them. "Here, would you like to have it?"

"Oh yes, thank you," Pam said as she pieced the two ends of the thunder egg together. "Our brother and sisters will love to see this."

Mr. Kinder glanced at his watch and Pete could see that the man wished them to leave.

"Well, thanks for all you've done, Mr. Kinder," Pete said.

"I'd show you more," their host replied, "but I have an appointment with a friend. I must go now."

Just then Casey stuck his big head in from the back room.

"Oh, that cat of mine," Mr. Kinder said. "He goes out the front and comes in the back. Now, Casey, you stay outdoors and hunt some mice until I return." The big yellow cat obediently pushed the screen door open and went out. Pete and Pam thanked the man again and took their leave.

They pedaled their bicycles home as fast as they could and found the other children in the garden with their mother. Pete showed them the thunder egg.

Delighted, little Sue took the two halves apart and peeked inside at the wonderful scenes inside it. "If it's a thunder egg, does it have lightning chickens?" she asked and everyone laughed.

Then Pete told about the Castle Rock quarry. Mrs. Hollister said that she had heard of it.

"I wish we could go out some day and see it," Pam remarked.

"Perhaps you can," her mother replied, "and sooner than you think. Daddy said that Indy had to make a delivery over that way this afternoon. Maybe he could take you."

Pete, Pam, Ricky and Holly were excited at the prospect of visiting the old quarry. Soon after lunch, Indy stopped with Mr. Hollister's truck. He had to deliver some paint several miles from Castle Rock Quarry.

"I'll drop them off there, Mrs. Hollister," Indy said, "and call for them when I return."

Ricky and Holly sat in front, while Pete and Pam made seats of the paint cans in the back of the truck. It took almost an hour to skirt the southern shore of Pine Lake and drive around to the hilly country behind it. Finally they came to a small side road with a faded sign saying: "Castle Rock Quarry."

"There it is!" Pete cried excitedly.

Indy turned in and drove along the winding, rutted road.

"Crickets, what a rough ride!" Pete said, the words coming out jerkily as he and Pam bounced on the paint cans in the back of the truck.

"I can see—why people don't—come out here much," his sister replied.

When they had gone almost a mile the road turned and ended suddenly. Before them was a wide rocky gap which opened into a huge hollowed-out hill. The truck stopped and the children hopped down and Indy followed.

"Yikes," said Ricky, awed, "they must have taken a lot of rock out of there."

The Hollisters advanced to the big opening and stared silently into the quarry.

The stony walls stood in an immense semicircle crowned by an emerald-green rim of trees. This curving cliff dropped several hundred feet to the floor below. Straight ahead, the back wall formed a precipice. The right side of the quarry, however, sloped gradually from the top.

On the far left was a sparkling little pond of greenish water. It extended nearly to the base of the steep stone cliff.

"Oh," Pam cried suddenly, "there's Castle Rock!" She pointed to the rim of the quarry above the pond. Silhouetted against the blue sky was a fantastic rock formation. There seemed to be a parapet and two turrets with windows in them.

"It *is* like a castle!" Holly exclaimed. "Oh, let's go up and play in it."

"No," Indy said quickly. "It's too dangerous. You might fall."

"We're always careful," Ricky assured him.

"No," their friend repeated firmly. "I'll be back in an hour and I want to find all of you waiting for me here—in one piece," he added, looking straight at Ricky. The children promised and Indy drove off.

"Crickets!" Pete said, "this is a spooky place!" Holding hands, they advanced slowly into the quarry. After they had walked several hundred feet,

21

they noticed a tall, rickety wooden building far to the right.

"That must have been where they crushed the stone," Pete reasoned.

"Let's take a look at it!" Ricky said and ran on ahead.

Following, the others saw him disappear around the side of the structure. As they approached, the old crushing mill loomed gray and forbidding. Turning the corner of it, they found a door hanging by one hinge. Ricky was standing on the threshold, looking inside. The others pressed close to him and peered into the dim interior. After being in the bright sunlight, it was hard for them to see anything.

Suddenly the youngsters gave a startled jump as a deep voice broke the stillness.

"What are you doing here?" asked a man standing behind them.

CHAPTER 3

A Curious Warning

THE children whirled about to see two men standing behind them.

"Crickets!" Pete said. "You frightened us. Where did you come from?"

"Never mind where we came from, where are you going?" asked one of the men. He was heavy-set, with a bulging middle and short, muscular arms. He had sandy hair, small, close-set eyes, and a large nose.

His companion was a short fellow, slightly balding. Large black-rimmed glasses seemed to cover most of his unsmiling face. Over his back he carried a knapsack and in his right hand he held a slender hammer.

"We're just looking around," Pete said, and told who they were. The stout man gave his name as Sid Raff. He said he had a few small rowboats on the quarry pond which he rented to fishermen.

The other man introduced himself as Wallace P. Ralston. "I'm a geologist," he explained stiffly.

"Oh, good," Pam said. "Then you know all about rocks, don't you?"

"I consider myself an expert," he replied without even a flicker of a smile.

"Would you look at this, please?" Pete asked, taking the bit of titanium from his pocket. "We thought there might be some in this quarry."

Ralston examined the stone closely through his large glasses. "I've never seen any of this around here."

"Then perhaps Mr. Kinder found it out West," Pete said.

"You know Mr. Kinder?" Sid Raff asked, cocking his head. "Nice fellow. You may look around the quarry, but don't get into any mischief."

"We won't," Ricky promised. The men started to walk away, but suddenly they turned and Raff said, "I'd advise you not to go near the pond."

"Oh, we can all swim," Holly piped up. "But we won't, 'cause we don't have our bathing suits."

Raff gave a short chuckle which shook his heavy shoulders. "You wouldn't dare to put a toe in that water," he said.

"Why?" asked Holly. "Would the fish bite us?"

"Worse than that," Ralston added. He waved his hammer toward the pond and went on. "Some fishermen said they saw a monster in there."

"That wouldn't bother us," Pete replied with a good-natured laugh, "because we don't believe in monsters."

At this, Sid Raff scowled. "It isn't funny," he

declared. "I've seen the monster myself!" With that, the pair strode toward the pond, at the edge of which the children saw two small rowboats tied to a stake.

"What's the big idea, I wonder?" Pete whispered to Pam, as the four youngsters walked over the gravelly quarry floor toward the cliff.

"They're trying to frighten us away, I guess," Pam replied.

"They must have a reason," Pete said. "Ricky, Holly, keep on the lookout for any bits of titanium."

Ricky put his head down like a hound dog on a scent. He zigzagged this way and that, looking for a gold-threaded rock. After a little while, he fell behind the others.

Pete, Pam and Holly walked slowly across the quarry. Now and then they stopped to gaze up at the tree-lined rim.

"Castle Rock is really beautiful," Pam said. "Oh, look," she added, pointing to the right. "There's a path leading to the top."

"Next time we come maybe we can climb up," Pete said hopefully. The three gazed longingly at the forbidden rock towers.

"Let's make it soon," Pam said eagerly.

As the children turned, Holly suddenly asked, "Where's Ricky?" They all scanned the huge quarry. The only persons to be seen were Raff and Ralston, sitting in one of the boats. Ricky was nowhere in sight.

Pete cupped his hands and called loudly. The sound echoed off the quarry walls, but there was no reply.

"Maybe he went back to that crushing mill," Pete suggested. "You know how he likes to explore things."

No sooner had the boy spoken when the sound of a crash came from the old wooden structure. Seconds later a thin, white plume of rock dust billowed up from the rickety roof.

Pete and Pam dashed toward the place like antelopes, with Holly at their heels, her pigtails flying out straight behind her. Reaching the doorway of the crushing mill, the children choked and coughed from the dust floating about.

"Ricky, Ricky, are you all right?" Pam shouted.

Leading the way, Pete stepped inside the gloomy building. Through a window high up on the side, a shaft of sunlight cast a ray on the opposite wall.

There was Ricky, standing on a narrow catwalk. A wooden stairway which he had climbed to the precarious perch had fallen down. Ricky, covered with white powder, was stranded, but did not appear to be hurt.

"I'm stuck!" he called down, and started to cough.

"Don't move," Pete shouted. "We'll get help!"

He hastened out of the door and nearly bumped into Raff and Ralston as they raced up to the old mill.

"Say, what's going on here?" Raff demanded. "Didn't I tell you kids to stay out of trouble?"

"We're sorry," Pete apologized.

"This old place is dangerous," Raff said.

"Will you please help us get him down?" Pam asked anxiously.

Without a word, Ralston opened his knapsack and pulled out a long, thin rope. Looping it in his hand, he hurled it up into the air toward Ricky. The first try missed, but on the second throw the redhead grabbed the end of the rope.

"Now, tie it securely to that catwalk," Ralston ordered, "and slide down."

Ricky knotted the rope. Then he grasped it with both hands, wrapped his legs around the strand, and slid down to the floor below.

"Yikes!" he said. "Thanks for saving me."

"You're welcome," Sid Raff said with a mock smile. Then his face turned stony. "Now, get out of the quarry and don't come back!"

"But, Mr. Kinder said—" Ricky began.

"I'll tell him all about you," Raff stormed. "Now scram!"

"Ricky, see what you did!" Holly whispered. "You've spoiled everything."

"I didn't know the old stairs were going to fall down," Ricky protested, as the four children walked out into the fresh air.

"You're safe, anyhow," Pam remarked. "Besides, it's nearly time for Indy to pick us up." They

"Yikes!"

stopped in the entrance to the quarry and looked back at Castle Rock.

"Crickets, I'd like to investigate that place," Pete said.

The Hollisters had walked only a few steps when Indy drove in with the truck. "Did you find what you were looking for?" he asked, as the children gathered around.

"We were looking for Ricky and we finally found him," Pete said, and as they drove home, Indy heard about their adventure.

"It sounds mysterious, all right," he told Pam. "I think you've run into another mystery."

For the rest of the day the Hollisters talked about the mysterious quarry, and Ricky wistfully said what a good place it would be to drop a parachute—if he had one.

This reminded Pete about the UFO. He was determined to look for the colored lights that night. But after supper heavy clouds gathered over the lake. Suddenly a strong gust of wind blew the screen door open, and they heard doors slamming in other parts of the house.

"Look how black the sky is!" Ricky exclaimed.

Lightning flashed, thunder cracked, and the downpour came. "Maybe it'll clear up," Pete said, but by bedtime it was still raining hard.

Before going to sleep, Pete set his alarm clock for 5 A.M. When it rang, he hopped out of bed. The rain had stopped.

After dressing quietly, Pete took a poncho blanket and tiptoed downstairs. Zip was sleeping in the kitchen.

"Shhh, quiet, boy," Pete said when the beautiful dog whined. "Don't wake anybody, 'cause I'm on the dawn patrol."

Zip accompanied his young master outdoors where Pete lay the poncho on the damp grass. It was still dark, but a thin sliver of light glowed on the eastern horizon. Pete lay on the blanket with Zip nuzzled close beside him and stared into the dark sky.

"If the colored lights are flying I can see them from here," he told himself. But in the hour that followed no unidentified objects appeared over Shoreham.

At the breakfast table Pete told the other children, "No UFO at dawn today. I watched from five o'clock until daylight."

"Why didn't you let me help you?" Ricky asked. "I'm good at finding colored lights in the sky."

Pete grinned. "You can help me this morning if you want. I'm going to the airport to see Jet Hawks. I want to ask him some questions about the lights he saw."

"Are the girls coming too?" Ricky asked with a sidewise glance at Holly.

The pigtailed girl turned her head to one side, placed her cereal spoon on the edge of her dish, looked very superior, and replied, "No. We have other plans."

Ricky was puzzled. "Is it some kind of a secret?" he asked.

"Yes," Sue answered briefly.

Ricky scratched his head and raised his eyebrows. "That's girls for you," he said to Pete. "Come on, let's get on our bikes. We have a secret meeting with a jet pilot."

Shoreham airport was several miles from the city and had grown large enough in recent years to accommodate small jet airplanes. But the two boys saw none as they pedaled up to the large airport building.

As they parked their bikes they saw a transport plane take off. The only other craft in the sky was a small, old-fashioned open-cockpit biplane which circled higher and higher.

"That's a real antique," Pete said, pausing to watch it. "I've seen pictures of those in books."

At the information desk inside the building Pete inquired for Jet Hawks. The attendant said that the pilot had just taken off.

"Oh, in that airliner, I'll bet," Ricky said.

The man smiled. "No. Jet's flying the biplane today. That's his hobby, you know. Fixing up old airplanes and flying them."

"Yikes, that's keen!" Ricky cried. "Is he coming back soon?"

The boys were told that the sportsman pilot

would be up for about half an hour. With that, Ricky and Pete hurried outside. They looked up into the sky to see the small biplane doing a barrel roll.

"Crickets!" Pete exclaimed. "Jet Hawks is an aerial acrobat!"

Craning their necks, they watched the plane loop the loop. After that it went into a nose dive and spun down through a white fluffy cloud.

"I'd love to be an airplane acrobat," Ricky said admiringly.

As the craft came lower the boys expected it to zoom up into another loop. Instead it kept heading toward the ground, spinning round and round.

Ricky clutched Pete's arm and cried, "Yikes! It's going to crash!"

CHAPTER 4

The Runaway Airplane

HOLDING their breath, Ricky and Pete watched the biplane spin toward the earth. It looked as if it would surely crash. But suddenly the nose turned upward and the plane went into a graceful roll. After making a low circle over the field, it landed close to one of the hangars.

When the single propeller had stopped spinning, out of the open cockpit stepped a very tall man. As Pete and Ricky hurried across the field they saw him take two wooden blocks from the ground beside the hangar and place them in front of the wheels. By the time the boys reached the flyer, he was tying the tail of the plane securely to a stake in the ground.

Seeing the wide-eyed pair watching him, he smiled. "Hi, fellows," he said in a friendly voice. "I bet you thought I was in trouble."

"You guessed it," Pete said. "Crickets, that was great flying!"

"Are you Jet Hawks?" Ricky asked.

"Why yes. Say, are you the boys who came to my house looking for me?" the pilot asked.

"I was there with my friend, Dave," Pete replied.

He introduced himself and Ricky. They both shook hands with the flyer.

"My wife said you asked for me," Jet said. "What can I do for you?"

"We heard from Mr. Kent that you saw a UFO," Pete explained. "We are interested in mysteries and would like to learn more about the strange lights."

"I was taking off for Chicago last Tuesday shortly before dawn," the flyer said. "After I was airborne, I saw these strange, colored lights off my starboard wing tip. They seemed to be descending, but I was going so fast that I lost sight of them in a few moments. I radioed the control tower but they could see nothing in the dark sky."

Pete inquired about the location of the flying object and was surprised to learn that Jet had seen it over the shore of Pine Lake close to where the Hollisters lived.

"Were the lights horizontal or vertical?" the older boy queried.

"They were one below the other," the pilot replied.

"Which might have meant," Pete reasoned, "that they were hanging from the end of a parachute."

"Perhaps," the pilot answered. "But the lights might have been part of a descending aircraft of some kind."

"Were they steady or blinking?" Ricky wanted to know.

"Blinking—on and off," Jet Hawks answered.

Then he put an arm around the shoulders of the two boys, and said with a chuckle, "You fellows are real detectives. Do you always play games like this?"

"We like to solve mysteries, Mr. Hawks," Pete replied.

"Just call me Jet," the pilot answered. "Everybody in the business does, and since you are doing work on the UFO mystery that makes you one of us."

"All right, Jet," Ricky said importantly. "Put it here!" He extended his right hand and the man pumped it in friendly fashion.

As he did, the pilot saw Pete look longingly at the biplane and said, "Say, would you all like to have a ride?"

"You bet!" the brothers exclaimed.

"Then come with me."

As the three walked toward the front of the small craft, Pete asked, "Why do you like antique airplanes, Jet?"

"Because they're fun," the pilot explained. "You can feel the wind in your face. Besides, I like to do somersaults in the sky."

"Can we do them, too?" Ricky asked brightly.

"I'm afraid not. But we'll do a little sightseeing just the same." Jet patted the side of the plane.

"Her name is *Spinning Jenny*," he told them, "and she was made in 1930."

"Yikes!" Ricky burst out. "In ancient times!"

"The plane's old all right, but very airworthy.

35

Come on," Jet said, as they walked around the trim little airplane. Pete saw that it had two open cockpits, one located under the top wing, the other slightly behind it.

"You'll ride in the front," Jet told them. "That cockpit is wide enough for two people. The plane has dual controls, so I can pilot it from the seat behind you."

"Crickets, I'd love to fly an airplane like that some day," Pete said.

"Who knows—you might," Jet replied. "Here, step on the wing and climb into the front seat."

"Oh, boy!" Pete exclaimed and did as he was told. Ricky followed. Pulling their legs over the edge of the cockpit, they sank down into a deep leather seat and faced an instrument panel. Between them was a stick, like a broom handle, which came up out of the bottom of the airplane.

"I've heard about a stick," Pete said, looking up at Jet who now was standing on the wing. "But I never thought it was a real one."

Jet smiled briefly, then looked serious. "You may help me start the plane," he said, "but you must do exactly what I tell you and be very careful."

"We will," Pete promised.

"This switch," Jet told them, pointing, "is the magneto. It is turned off now and must stay there while I give the propeller a couple of easy turns. Then when I tell you, turn the switch on, and I will swing the prop."

36

Next, the pilot pulled the stick back as far as it would go and secured it with one of the two seat belts.

"Now, Pete, listen carefully," he said. "After I pull through the prop several times to prime the engine, I want you to crack the throttle just a little. About half an inch." He showed Pete exactly what to do. "This will make the engine idle at a slow rate. Then I'll untie the tail and unchock the wheels. Finally, I'll climb in and we'll be ready to fly."

The brothers tingled with excitement as the pilot stepped in front of the airplane, reached with his long arms and grasped the end of the propeller. He flipped it once, then twice.

"Okay, Pete," he called out. "Crack the throttle!"

Pete advanced it half an inch. Jet swung the propeller and the single engine throbbed to life.

"Good boy!" Jet sang out above the noise. "Sit tight now and don't touch anything!"

The pilot walked around to the rear of the plane and started to untie the rope holding the tail. Ricky strained his neck to watch, but the cockpit was too deep. Curious, the boy raised himself to get a better look.

"Sit still!" Pete cautioned.

As Ricky plopped down again, his hand hit the throttle. At that instant Jet Hawks untied the tail.

With a sudden roar the airplane jumped the wooden blocks and raced ahead!

Pete and Ricky were speechless with fright, as the tail of the plane lifted. Pete glanced back to see Jet Hawks racing madly after his runaway airplane, but it was going too fast for him.

The wind whistled through the struts and the racket of the motor drowned out the lads' cries of dismay. Ricky's first impulse was to climb out, but Pete restrained him.

"Sit tight!" he ordered. "We're safer here!" As he pulled Ricky back into the cockpit, the safety belt jumped from the stick and it sprang forward.

Then the most amazing thing happened! The boys could no longer feel the roll of the wheels on the concrete runway. They looked down and saw the ground dropping away beneath them.

They were flying!

Pete opened his mouth and gasped. The rushing wind nearly took away his breath.

"What are we going to do!" Ricky yelled over the roar of the motor. Far below he could see Jet Hawks waving frantically.

Suddenly Pete had an idea. He reached across the cockpit and shut off the throttle. The motor stopped and all that could be heard was the eerie whistling of the wind through the struts. I've heard that sometimes these small planes can land by themselves, Pete thought. I hope so! He leaned over and shouted into Ricky's ear, "Sit still and

They were flying.

don't touch the stick! I think we'll make it all right."

The plane nosed into a gentle glide, coming lower and lower. It cleared the airport boundary and began to descend into a small clearing.

"Hang on!" Pete shouted.

The wheels brushed against the tops of some small trees, then with a bump, bump, bump settled down into the rough ground and stopped.

"Yikes!" Ricky said and both boys slumped back into the seat. As they relaxed, the wail of a siren sounded in the distance, and in a few moments a truck from the airport, its cab light flashing red, streaked across the runway into the clearing. It bounced over the ruts and came to a stop beside the boys. Out leaped Jet Hawks and an airport attendant.

"Are you all right, boys?" the pilot cried.

"We're okay," Pete replied with a weak grin. Pale-faced, the two men helped the brothers out of the cockpit.

Jet managed a wry smile. "You boys told me you were detectives, not flyers!"

"I—I'm sorry," Ricky said. "I didn't sit still. It was all my fault. Pete's the one who saved us."

"Shutting off the throttle was quick thinking," Jet said. "Well, no harm done," he added, and the attendant winced. "You landed safely and the old crate's okay."

Ricky was relieved not to get the scolding he

knew he deserved. "We'll be better next time, Jet," Pete said.

"I think that's enough for today," the pilot replied firmly. "We'll tow *Jenny* back to the airport." A few minutes later a rope had been secured to the front of the plane and the truck pulled it back across the airport to where the young flyers had taken off.

Jet and the attendant put the plane into the hangar while the boys waited outside. As the men emerged a station wagon drove up beside the main building. The horn beeped twice and Jet waved to a pretty woman seated at the wheel, a girl beside her.

"My wife and daughter," Jet said. "Come on over and meet them."

By now Ricky's hands had quit trembling and the butterflies in Pete's stomach had settled down. Both boys looked calm enough as they were introduced to Jet's wife, Isobel.

"I've already met Pete," she said with a smile, "and I'm glad to know you, too, Ricky. This is our daughter, Daphne." The little girl was about ten years old and had pretty flaxen hair and a dimple in her cheek.

Jet winked at the boys. "We call her Daffy for short."

Pete and Ricky smiled and Daffy smiled back. "Did Daddy give you a ride in *Spinning Jenny*?" she asked sweetly.

Pete merely gulped and nodded his head.

"I'll say they had a ride!" Jet exclaimed. "I'll tell you about it as we drive them home."

"What about our bikes?" Ricky asked.

"Put them in the back," Jet ordered, "and climb into the rear seat."

The boys obeyed. The pilot slipped behind the wheel of the car, and they headed for Shoreham.

While Jet Hawks told the story of the flying adventure, his wife listened horrified. But Daffy's eyes sparkled. "How wonderful!" she exclaimed. "Ricky and Pete, you'll be spacemen yet."

It was nearly lunch time when Jet Hawks pulled up in front of the Hollister home.

"You must meet our family," Pete said, and hurried into the house to get his mother.

While Ricky unloaded the bicycles, Mrs. Hollister and her daughters came out of the house. They introduced themselves and before long the girls were chattering happily with Daffy. Mrs. Hollister invited the Hawkses to have lunch.

"We really shouldn't impose upon you," the pilot said, looking somewhat embarrassed, "but I have a long story to tell about our adventure, and this will be a good time to do it."

After dessert the children were excused from the table and a few minutes later the grownups joined them in the living room. The four girls huddled on the sofa and Pete heard Holly whisper the word "secret" to Daffy.

"What were you doing while Rick and I were away?" he asked.

Pam looked at Ricky and said, "We made something this morning." Then she gave Sue a little push and the girl ran upstairs.

"It's especially for you, Ricky," Holly declared.

A minute later Sue returned, her hands full of colored paper doll clothes. Ricky looked startled. "Are these for me?" he asked, his face growing beet red.

CHAPTER 5

A Spooky Discovery

"DOLL clothes for me!" Ricky exclaimed, making a wry face. "You must be joking."

When everyone laughed, Pam quickly said, "Oh, Sue, that's not what I wanted you to bring down. You know—the other thing."

Sue scooted upstairs on hands and feet. This time she returned carrying a huge folded parachute. Ricky's eyes lighted up when he saw it and he grinned broadly.

The chute was made of heavy white paper and the sections were neatly sewn. "This is keen! Thanks!" Ricky exclaimed, as he took the gift.

"All of us girls helped to make it," Pam said. "That was our secret!"

"Crickets!" Pete exclaimed. "Now we can go to Castle Rock again and drop the parachute!"

Mrs. Hollister suggested a picnic at the quarry the following afternoon. She invited the Hawkses, but Jet had a flight to make. However, his wife and Daffy accepted.

"My husband has some work, too," Mrs. Hollister said, smiling at Mrs. Hawks, "so we'll go with the children."

After their guests had left, Ricky and Holly practiced dropping the parachute from the garage roof. Joey Brill did not show up to annoy them. The only one who watched was Domingo. Pete had let the burro out of the barn to graze on the sweet grass of the lawn, and whenever the chute dropped, Domingo raised his head and gave a loud "Ee-aw."

After supper that night Pete told Pam that it would be best to look for the mysterious lights just before dawn, because that was when Jet had seen them.

"I'll set my alarm and get up early," Pete said. "If I see anything suspicious, I'll call you."

It was almost morning when the alarm bell tinkled. Pete dressed rapidly and tiptoed downstairs. A few minutes later he spread a tarpaulin beside the dock and watched the black sky.

He had been looking into the darkness for a few minutes when something swooped past him. Pete jumped and his heart pounded.

"It's only a bat," he said to himself. "Crickets, I must be getting jittery."

As Pete watched the sky again, suddenly a blue light trailed down out of the darkness. It turned green, then purple, and disappeared in the woods not far from the Hollister home.

"No, I'm not dreaming!" Pete told himself. He scrambled to his feet, hurried beneath Pam's window, and called to her. A few minutes later the

45

screen door opened quietly and Pam came out holding Zip by his collar.

"We'll take him with us just in case," she whispered.

Pete and Pam mounted their bicycles, switched on the headlights, and pedaled out of the driveway. The pebbles beneath their wheels sounded noisy in the still of the early dawn, and the damp, cool air rushed past their faces as they sped down the street toward the patch of woods where the mysterious lights had disappeared.

After a few minutes Pete stopped in front of an empty lot which led to the woods along the lake shore. "Here's where I saw the thing come down, Pam," he said. They dismounted and went on foot.

Although dawn was lighting the sky above them, it was dim and gloomy among the trees. Birds were just awakening, and in the distance an owl hooted mournfully before settling down for the day.

"Do you think we'd better go back now?" Pam asked as they reached the middle of the woods.

"No, I'm sure the thing landed in here," Pete said softly. "Let's start walking in circles."

"What are we looking for?" Pam whispered.

Pete confessed that he did not really know. "There were lights, that's all," he said.

Zip had ranged far and wide in front of them. Now he returned and gave a sharp bark.

"What is it, boy?" Pete asked. "Did you find something?"

The dog circled around, then stalked toward a thicket, raising each paw carefully and sniffing. Pete and Pam followed until their pet came to a complete halt. Then he crouched low and growled. A chill of fright tingled Pam's spine as a deep voice came from the brush.

"Send me to Post Office Box 48 in Shoreham," it said.

Pete stared at the bushes in disbelief. The voice repeated the message. Zip barked and bounded forward, but no one was in sight. *Where did the voice come from?* Pete asked himself as he pressed forward.

All at once the words came again—almost beneath their feet. Pam jumped. She was almost standing on a small box. Attached to it and nearly hidden by the brush was a white paper parachute and between the two was a string of colored lights.

As Pete bent down to pick up the box, the voice spoke again. "It's a recording device," he said and pushed a tiny switch. The voice stopped.

"This is the UFO all right," Pam said as she examined the strings which held the little box to the chute. "Here are the lights." She pointed to a row of colored bulbs on one of the cords.

"Whoever dropped this parachute wants someone to find it," Pete reasoned.

"But why send it to Post Office Box 48 in Shoreham?" Pam asked, perplexed.

47

With Pete carefully carrying the contraption, the brother and sister cycled home. Mrs. Hollister was preparing breakfast when they hurried into the house to announce their find.

"This is an ingenious invention," Mr. Hollister said after he had examined it.

"But what's it for?" Holly asked.

"Perhaps to attract attention to things that are dropped by parachute," Pam said.

After breakfast Pete telephoned Dave to tell him of their spooky discovery. Then the two boys and Pam went to Mr. Kent's house to show him the talking parachute.

The editor moved the Sunday papers from the sofa and asked them to sit down. "So you've found what the UFO is," he said. "Congratulations! Now all you have to do is solve the mystery of who's dropping these things, and why."

"If we can learn who rents Post Office Box 48 we can ask him about it," Pete remarked.

"You won't find out as simply as that," Mr. Kent replied. "Post office boxes are private. The postmaster will not tell you who rents number forty-eight."

"We're going to mail the invention first thing in the morning," Pam said. "We can keep watch and see who comes to get it."

Mr. Kent wished them luck and said he would put a story in the paper asking the mysterious inventor to come forward.

After promising to keep the editor informed, the children hurried home to get ready for church. When they had returned and eaten a snack, Mrs. Hollister prepared the picnic food. All was ready by the time Daffy and her mother arrived in the middle of the afternoon, and the Hollisters eagerly told about finding the talking parachute.

"How wonderful!" Daffy said. "Wait till Daddy hears about this!"

The ride to the quarry road was smooth, but from there on it was bumpy fun. Soon the picnickers turned off on a narrow lane which Mrs. Hollister said would lead to the rim of the quarry. They drove uphill until the road ended in a clearing.

"There's Castle Rock!" Pam exclaimed.

"Let's go inside!" Holly said, as she jumped out of the car. The others quickly followed her to the wonderful rock formation.

"Oh," said Daffy, "it looks like a fairyland castle!"

Before them rose two ivy-covered stone turrets, with a rocky parapet between. One tower was solid rock but in the other was a narrow doorway. The picnickers entered and found themselves in a large, round chamber with a wide window. Through it they looked out on the quarry and the pond far below.

"Erosion from the wind and rain caused this castle formation," Mrs. Hollister told them. After cautioning the children to be careful, she and Mrs. Hawks went outside.

"Let's drop the parachute," Ricky said eagerly. He sat down on a large boulder near the window to untangle the strings of his chute.

"I'll go down and catch it for you, Ricky," Holly volunteered.

"All right," her brother said. "The next time you can drop it down to me."

Holly found the steep trail and scrambled far down into the quarry below. The others watched her from the big window in the turret. Holly scampered to the thin strip of ground between the tower and the pond and called up, "Drop it, Ricky!"

Her brother flung the parachute far out from the face of the cliff. It opened and floated down, down, down. Holly raced over and grabbed it before it could touch the ground.

"Good catch," Daffy cried out and clapped her hands. "Oh, what fun!"

Holly folded the parachute and scrambled up the trail like a little monkey. When she reached the top Pam said, "You drop it now. Ricky and I will go down and catch it."

When they reached the bottom, however, the wind suddenly freshened, blowing in the direction of the pond, so Pam and Ricky ran closer to the edge of the water. They looked up to see Holly twirling the parachute. It sailed out from the cliff,

Holly grabbed it

billowed, and floated down, dropping closer and closer to the pond.

Pam and Ricky backed up, keeping their eyes glued to the chute. High on the rim, the rest of the children shouted and waved their arms. But Pam did not realize this was a warning.

She stepped backward right into the pond and, with a gasp, disappeared beneath the cold water. Fighting her way to the surface, Pam touched a large object with her foot. It wriggled out of the way!

The monster! she thought.

CHAPTER 6

Knights and a Dragon

KICKING wildly, Pam swam toward the surface. When her head popped above water, she took a deep breath of fresh air and hoisted herself over the rocky rim of the pond.

Ricky, who had caught the parachute, saw his sister's look of fright. "What's the matter?" he asked. "You only got wet."

"My feet touched something big and wriggly," Pam said.

"The monster!" Ricky exclaimed.

"For a second I thought so, too," Pam admitted. "I know it *couldn't* have been a monster, but all the same, I don't want to go swimming in there again."

"Yikes, you said it!" Ricky agreed.

The heat of the bright sun started to dry Pam's clothes even as she and Ricky headed for the trail. But they had not gone far when the boy's keen eyes spied something bright near the foot of the cliff. He and Pam went to investigate.

"It's an old piece of machinery," Pam said.

Ricky hunkered down to examine a circular gadget with a rusty motor attached. A pipe led from it to the edge of the pond, and it was a shiny fitting that had caught his eye.

"This is a pump," Pam said. "It probably was used years ago to keep the quarry drained of water."

As the children poked about the old machine, they heard a noise and looked up to see Sid Raff at their side.

"You're back again, eh?" he asked the surprised Hollisters. "What are you doing with that pump?"

"Just l-looking at it," Ricky replied.

"We came for a picnic today," Pam said, and pointed up to the Castle Rock.

"Well, the pump is broken," Raff declared. "It doesn't work, so don't fuss with it. I don't mind if you have a picnic up there," he added, gesturing toward the rim of the quarry, "but I would advise you to stay away from here."

"Why?" Ricky asked.

"Because there was a landslide here night before last." Raff pointed to a jumble of rocks and gravel at the base of the cliff not far from where they were standing.

"It's dangerous," the man went on. "You children ought not to play around the quarry."

"Thank you for telling us," Pam said politely. She took Ricky by the hand and started to climb up the stony trail toward the top of the cliff. After a few minutes they looked back. Sid Raff was gone.

"He must be a magician the way he vanishes," Ricky said.

"Where did he come from in the first place?" Pam asked.

Ricky shrugged, and they continued climbing the precipitous trail. As they skirted around the landslide section which Raff had pointed out, Pam said, "Maybe Raff is all right, and just doesn't want to see us get hurt."

As she spoke, Ricky reached down to pick up a tiny stone. It was threaded with lines of gold. "See what I found!" he said proudly.

"That looks like titanium!" Pam exclaimed.

"But Sid Raff told us there wasn't any around here."

"The landslide could have unearthed a vein of it!" Pam replied excitedly. "Wait until we tell Mr. Kinder! This might make his quarry very valuable."

"I'll bet that geologist fellow would like to know about it, too," Ricky declared, putting the stone in his pocket.

By the time they had reached the rim, their mother, Mrs. Hawks and the girls had spread a picnic lunch in the shade of a pine tree near the Castle Rock.

"Are you dried out, dear?" Mrs. Hollister asked Pam. "We saw your accident."

"And what did Sid Raff have to say?" was Pete's query.

When Pam and Ricky had told their story, Mrs. Hawks said with a smile, "I'm sure it wasn't a monster you touched, Pam."

"But that was a piece of titanium that Ricky found," Pete said. "Now Mr. Kinder can sell his quarry for a high price!"

"Or work it himself," Daffy declared.

"Let's show him the stone first thing in the morning," Holly suggested.

After they had finished eating the delicious picnic supper, Daffy and Pam skipped rope with Sue and Holly. Pete and Ricky stood looking out of the castle window at the pond below.

The place was empty and quiet as long shadows crept over the quarry. Pete was standing deep in thought about the day's adventure, when Daffy tapped him on the shoulder and said, "Would you like to play knights and ladies with us?"

"All right," said Pete, grinning, "but if I'm a knight, I'm going off to the wars."

"I want to play knights and ladies, too," Sue declared. "I'll be the queen."

Pam agreed to be the queen's mother and Daffy, the lady-in-waiting. Holly insisted upon being a knight. She would join Ricky and Pete in fighting off the dragon attacking the castle.

While Pete found some broken tree branches suitable for swords, Sue seated herself on the round rock near the castle window. Pam draped the picnic cloth around her for a robe. Daffy quickly made Sue a crown from a turned-up paper plate and tied it on her head with string. After fastening plate

"What would Your Majesty desire?"

coronets to their own heads, Pam and Daffy stood beside Sue.

The two mothers looked on, amused, as Daffy curtsied to Sue and said, "What would Your Majesty most desire?"

"Slay the dragon and bring his head to me!"

"Oh dear, Your Majesty!" Pam exclaimed. "That sounds bloodthirsty."

"It says so in my fairy tale book," Sue protested. "Besides it's only 'maginary."

All the while Ricky had been observing Sue's throne rock. He thought it looked as if it were covering a hole in the floor, but before he could say anything Sue cried out, "Here comes Pete with your swords."

Pete handed a stick to Ricky and Holly and kept one for himself.

"There's the dragon lurking in the trees," Pete said, pointing to a stand of stately pines.

The three dashed out for the attack. Their wooden swords darted in and out trying to snick off the imaginary dragon's head.

"He's breathing fire on us!" Ricky cried and retreated several steps. The others followed him.

"He'll devour us all!" Holly screeched.

The three trusty defenders of Queen Sue retreated step by step, fighting vainly to dispatch the onrushing dragon. Finally, when they were nearly to the throne, Pete lunged forward with his sword and struck the make-believe dragon in the heart. The great beast rolled to the ground.

"You got him, Sir Pete!" Pam cried out.

"Now off with his head!" Sue commanded.

Ricky went *zing zing* and then held up the dragon's head while Holly leaned weakly against the rock window. She turned to look down at the quarry, then suddenly gave a chilling shriek.

"Oh look, there's a real dragon!"

The others dashed to her side and looked down at the pond below. Nothing could be seen but a big swirl on the surface of the dark waters.

"It must be the same monster Pam touched," Ricky cried out.

Mrs. Hollister suggested that it might have been a large fish that had come to the surface to feed on bugs.

"You're probably right, Mother," Pete said. "Anyhow, let's get rid of Sue's dragon." With much merriment, Pete and Ricky struggled to lift the imaginary beast. They pulled it to the edge of the cliff and threw it over.

"There," said Sue, "the queen is safe at last."

Soon afterward the picknickers climbed into the station wagon for the ride back to Shoreham.

"Everybody accounted for?" asked Mrs. Hollister, looking back over her shoulder.

"Count off," Pete ordered, and each child sang out his name.

Suddenly Mrs. Hollister made a face and said,

"Come, boys. Which one of you took the car keys?"

"Not I," Pete declared.

"Me neither," said Ricky.

Their mother looked puzzled. "I'm sure I left the keys in the car," she said. "Now they're gone! Somebody must have taken them!"

CHAPTER 7

A Lonely Cat

"MAY we stay here all night?" Ricky asked hopefully as his mother vainly rummaged in her purse for the car keys.

"We're going to find the keys, and then drive home," Mrs. Hollister said with determination. "I had them in a leather case. They couldn't just have walked off!"

"Somebody might have taken them on purpose," Pete said. "We didn't have our eyes on the car all the time."

"Who would play such a trick?" Daffy's mother asked.

"Possibly Raff or Ralston," Ricky said.

"They didn't seem like jokers to me," Pam remarked.

"Nevertheless, we must all look about carefully," Mrs. Hollister said, "before it gets dark."

The grownups and children got out of the car and started to search for the keys in ever-widening circles.

"No luck," said Pam with a sigh as they finished scanning the clearing where the station wagon stood.

61

Suddenly Sue, who had wandered near the edge of the woods, cried out, "I found them. Here they are!"

The others raced over to where the little girl was removing the keys from the side of a small tree, to which the case had been fastened by a thumbtack. And much to the surprise of all, a white piece of paper fell to the ground. Pam picked it up and unfolded the paper. On it was scrawled:

WARNING.
STAY AWAY FROM CASTLE ROCK!

"Oh, this is terrible," Mrs. Hollister said.

"There's something mighty mysterious going on," Mrs. Hawks added.

"And we'll get to the bottom of it!" Pete vowed. "Nobody's going to scare us away."

As they drove from the quarry, Pam felt that strange eyes were peering at them, but they saw no one. Most of the way back, the picnickers tried to guess who might have played the mean trick, and why the warning was given.

"It's just somebody's idea of fun," Daffy said finally, and the girls changed to the subject of dolls.

"I'm always going to have dolls," Pam said, "even when I'm grown up."

Daffy said that she loved them, too, and liked nothing better than to play house with her toys.

"Poor Maddie-Poo," Sue declared. "She's sick." Maddie-Poo was one of her favorites. Something had happened to Maddie-Poo's head, so that it had become loose. It would flop from side to side, and remained straight only when Maddie-Poo was put in her doll crib.

The girls' chatter about dolls came to an end when they arrived at the Hollisters' home. Mrs. Hawks and Daffy said good-by, thanking the Hollisters for a happy afternoon. The younger children, tired from an exciting day, went to bed early, while Pete and Pam discussed their plans for the following morning.

"We'll mail the talking parachute to Post Office Box 48," Pete said. "Let's enclose a letter asking the owner to get in touch with us, so we can clear up the mystery of the strange parachute."

"Good idea," Pam agreed. "And Daffy will tell her father that we found the UFO," she added.

It was decided that after mailing the parachute box, Pete and Pam would go to Mr. Kinder's house and show him the stone with the gold threads that Ricky had found in the quarry.

"He'll be thrilled with the good news!" Pam said happily.

On the way to his store next morning, Mr. Hollister drove Pete and Pam to the post office. After the talking box had been mailed, the children walked over to Mr. Kinder's place. The front door was closed. Pete rang the bell and they waited for a few minutes, but no one answered it.

"I guess he's not at home," Pete said. "Maybe he's gone on one of his trips again."

Just then Casey came from around the corner of the house, leaped over the porch rail, and rubbed against Pete's leg. Then the tomcat yowled loudly.

"That's funny," Pam said. "If Mr. Kinder went on a trip, surely he would have taken Casey with him."

"This old cat's hungry," Pete said. "What say we feed him? I don't think White Nose and her kittens will mind."

Casey followed them eagerly, and even though it was a long walk, he marched behind Pete and Pam all the way to their home.

The big cat followed them into the kitchen where White Nose was lapping some milk with her tiny brood. When she saw Casey, White Nose licked the white drops from her whiskers and led her family down the steps to the basement.

"White Nose is unfriendly," observed Holly as she watched her pet snub the new arrival.

"They really haven't had the proper introduction," Pete said with a chuckle. Then he went to the pantry and returned with a can of cat food. He opened the tin and set it before Mr. Kinder's tomcat.

Casey ate as if he had not been fed in a week! After gobbling all the food he turned to the dish of milk White Nose had left and lapped it up too. Then he meowed his thanks, pushed the screen door open, and ran into the yard.

"Come back," Holly said running after him, but

Casey bounded toward the sidewalk and disappeared down the street.

"He'll find his way home all right," Pete said. "Cats always do."

Pam was occupied with thoughts about why Mr. Kinder would leave poor Casey when she was interrupted by a telephone call. It was Daffy. She invited the Hollister girls to come over after lunch.

"Please bring your dolls," Daffy said. "We can have fun playing house."

When Holly and Sue heard the news they were very happy. "Oh," the little dark-haired girl said skipping about, "I'll take Maddie-Poo, too. We can play hospital with her."

When luncheon was over the three girls collected their dolls. Maddie-Poo was put in a small doll carriage and the rest of the assortment, including rag dolls, china dolls and Pam's collection from foreign countries, were placed neatly in Ricky's coaster wagon.

"Pay no attention to Joey Brill if you should see him," Mrs. Hollister cautioned as the girls departed down the street.

"We won't," Pam promised.

It was a long walk to Daffy's house but the day was bright and the air cool. Occasionally Sue would stop and feel Maddie-Poo's cheek, but her doll was not feverish, and Sue declared that she could take the trip without any trouble.

When they passed Joey's house the girls looked

neither right nor left but kept eyes straight ahead. Daffy lived near the end of the block. She met them in the front of her house and showed her new friends into the back yard.

"This is keen," Holly said as she observed the green lawn and all the things that belonged to Daffy. She had a swing, a seesaw, a bright, shiny slide and monkey bars.

Leaving her dolls, Holly did not know which of the contraptions to try out first. She ran over to the swing, pumped back and forth for a minute, then jumped off and climbed the monkey bars. Pam gave Sue a ride on the seesaw.

"I want to try the slide," Sue declared after a few ups and downs. She scooted up the ladder, but instead of sitting down on the slide, Sue decided to go down head first on her back.

"Oh, look out!" Pam warned her.

Sue slid all the way down, landing with a plop on the soft grass, and doing a backward somersault.

"You're an imp!" Pam told her, as she brushed the back of her shorts. "Come now, let's play with the dolls."

In one corner of the yard stood a small cherry tree which provided a little circle of shade. After laying a pink doll blanket on the ground, Daffy went into the house and returned with an armful of dolls. Then she brought out a small table and chairs, along with a tiny set of dishes.

"Oh this is great fun!" Holly declared as she

"Oh, look out!"

helped put the dolls around it in various positions.

Carefully Sue lifted Maddie-Poo out of the doll carriage and cuddled her gently. "There, there, don't cry," she said soothingly. "Your head will grow fast again, Maddie-Poo."

Sue arranged several handfuls of green grass as a pillow for Maddie-Poo and put her down gently.

After all the dolls had been fed, and as they were being put to bed by their mothers, Holly suddenly pointed down the row of back yards to a tall tree at the rear of Joey's house. "Look!" she called out. "Joey and Will are trying to fly Ricky's parachute."

The two boys had climbed to the top branches of the tree. In one hand Joey held the orange parachute. As the girls looked on, he flung it out as far as he could. The chute soared into the air, but in coming down caught onto a telephone wire leading into the Brill's home.

Holly giggled. "It serves them right," she declared.

Joey and Will climbed down and got a long rope with which Joey made a lasso. But he could not snare the parachute. Instead, the rope tangled with the telephone wire.

Joey and Will both tugged. Down came the parachute—and the telephone wire with it!

"Oh," Pam said. "They'll get in trouble for that."

Instantly Mrs. Brill appeared at the back door and scolded the boys. She said she would have to go next door and inform the telephone company.

When she had gone Will Wilson stuck his tongue out at the girls.

Holly said, "Poo," then went back to playing with the dolls. Now they were all safely tucked in bed, even Maddie-Poo whose eyes were closed.

"She's sleeping quietly," Sue remarked, as Mrs. Hawks called them inside to ice cream and cake.

Only Holly lingered to be certain that Maddie-Poo was comfortable. The other girls skipped into the house and sat down to a table decorated with a colorful paper cloth. On it were plates of ice cream and white cake with chocolate icing.

"Hurry, Holly, before your ice cream melts," Daffy called.

Holly did not reply immediately. But seconds later her voice came loud and clear. "Help! Help!" she cried.

CHAPTER 8

The Kidnaped Doll

HEARING Holly's cries, Daffy dashed to the window and looked out. "Oh!" she exclaimed. "Poor Holly!" The pigtailed girl was standing on tiptoes with her braids tied to one of the monkey bars.

"Wait, Holly!" Daffy cried out. "We'll help you get loose."

They all ran outside and Pam quickly untied her sister's braids. Holly said Will and Joey had done this.

"Those meanies!" said Daffy.

"Joey and Will also took our dolls!" Holly said with hot tears running down her cheeks. She explained that the boys had sneaked up in back of her, tied her by the hair, scooped up the dolls, and raced off through the adjoining back yards. Now they were nowhere in sight.

"Where did they go?" asked Mrs. Hawks, who had run into the yard to see what the fuss was all about.

"Maddie-Poo will get hurted even worse!" Sue wailed.

"Come on," Pam said. "Follow me, we'll get our dolls back."

The four girls ran from one back yard to the next. On the way they picked up their dolls, which were scattered here and there. Because of the soft grass none of them were broken, but their hair was disheveled, and their pretty dresses mussed.

By the time the playmates reached Joey Brill's back yard they had recovered all of their precious children except Maddie-Poo.

"Where's my dolly! I want Maddie!" Sue clamored.

"Oh dear, there she is!" Holly cried out, pointing up into the tree from which Joey and Will had launched the parachute. There was Maddie-Poo, hanging head down by one leg.

"Those horrid boys threw her up there," Daffy guessed, "and now she's stuck."

As the wind stirred the leaves, Maddie-Poo swung back and forth with her head flopping worse than ever. The girls stood beneath the kidnaped doll waiting for Maddie to fall from the tree at any moment.

Just then a smiling man came into the yard with a long ladder. "Is this where the telephone line is down?" he asked. But before they could answer, the repairman spied the dangling doll. "I'll get her for you," he offered, and set his ladder against the tree. Climbing very carefully so as not to disturb Maddie, the telephone man rescued Sue's doll. As he did,

"I'll get her for you," he offered.

Mrs. Brill came out into the yard and saw him.

"How did the doll get into the tree?" she asked.

The girls explained what had happened.

"I'm sorry that Joey did this," Mrs. Brill said. "Is your baby badly hurt?"

Sue told her that Maddie's neck was a little crooked before the kidnaping, but now it flopped terribly. Besides, one of her legs had been nearly pulled off.

"Let me take her," Joey's mother offered kindly. "I know of a good doll hospital where Maddie-Poo can be fixed."

The children thanked Mrs. Brill and the man, who quickly went about repairing the fallen telephone wire. "Is this your parachute?" he asked the girls.

Pam said it had belonged to her brother, but Joey Brill could keep it because Ricky had another one.

With their arms full of dolls, the four playmates returned to Daffy's house. Mrs. Hawks had put their ice cream in the freezer. Now she brought it out.

"Yummy, it's awful good," Holly said as she spooned a big blob of chocolate into her mouth.

"I'm so sorry those rough boys spoiled your fun," Daffy's mother said as she served them each a second piece of cake.

After the refreshments had been eaten, the girls cleared the table, then set about to freshen up their dolls. Daffy and Holly washed their dresses with soap and water, while Pam and Sue rearranged the dolls' hair. Afterward the girls took turns pressing the little frocks with Daffy's toy iron.

"Thank you very much, Mrs. Hawks," Pam said when the party was over. "It was such fun."

"Come back again," Daffy's mother replied as she patted Sue on the head. Holly and Pam loaded the dolls into the coaster wagon, but Sue preferred to wheel her carriage empty. No doll could take the place of Maddie-Poo.

Although Pam kept a sharp lookout for Joey Brill, the bully did not show himself on the way back to the Hollister house. When the girls arrived, Pete and Ricky were sitting on the front porch steps and Mrs. Hollister was watering her roses. The boys were indignant when they heard what Joey and Will had done to their sisters.

"They'd better look out if I catch them," Pete said hotly.

Mrs. Hollister overheard this and said, "Pete, I don't want any fighting with Joey Brill or Will Wilson."

"All right, Mother," Pete said reluctantly, "but I have a thing or two to tell them the next time we meet."

It was not until the following day that Pete saw the doll kidnaper. The children had arisen early and at the breakfast table had discussed the next move in their search for the parachute man.

"I'd suggest that we watch the post office in pairs," Pete said. "The man is sure to come to Box 48 for his package sooner or later. Then we can ask him about his new invention."

"If you find him," Mr. Hollister said, "I'm sure the newspaper would be glad to print his story."

It was agreed that Ricky meet Dave Mead. Together the two boys could observe the post office boxes until noon, at which time they would be replaced by whoever was available to keep up the watch.

"Fine," Mr. Hollister said. "That leaves you to cut the grass, Pete."

"And I'll trim the edges," Holly volunteered.

When Ricky set off, Pam helped her mother with household chores. Sue skipped to the front sidewalk where she waited for the postman, as she often did. Sometimes he brought her a lollipop, which made getting the mail even more fun.

Pete had started the power mower, cutting neat swaths in the green lawn, when Holly spied Mr. Barnes, the mailman, far down the street. He approached the Hollisters' place slowly, whistling a merry tune. Just then Joey Brill drove past on his bicycle.

"Go away, you mean Joey!" Sue called out.

Pete heard her protest above the noisy mower, shut it off, and he and Holly ran to the sidewalk. Joey was circling around in the street.

"I got even with you!" Joey taunted.

75

Pete looked calmly at the bully and said, "I hear you and Will like to play with dolls." This made Holly giggle.

"No, we don't," Joey retorted.

"You were seen running away with an armful," Pete went on. "Isn't that right, Sue?" The girl nodded vigorously, and Pete continued, "Why don't you go in the house and get a doll for my friend."

Joey's face flushed, and he pedaled around in circles furiously, trying to think of a retort to Pete's teasing. But as he swooped by, the front wheel struck the curb, throwing the bicycle out of control. It veered onto the sidewalk and hit the postman.

"Ow!" Mr. Barnes cried. The mailman, Joey and the bicycle went down while dozens of letters flew in all directions.

The bully mumbled a weak apology, picked up his bicycle, and raced off as fast as he could. Pete, meanwhile, helped the postman to his feet, and Holly and Sue collected the scattered mail.

"Oh, that pesky boy," Mr. Barnes said as he brushed off his uniform. Holly handed him the mail they had rescued and he thanked the children for their aid.

"Do you have some letters for us?" Sue chirped sweetly, as if nothing had happened.

"Hmm, yes, I do," came the reply. The postman sorted some envelopes and handed them to her. Sue made-believe read them, then handed the letters to Pete. "Is there something for me?" she asked.

"Here's a letter for all of us," Pete replied. Then he let out a surprised cry and said, "It's from Hootnanny Gandy! Remember him?"

Hootnanny was a special friend of the Hollisters whom they had met on an adventure in New York City. Pete recalled him as a tall, thin old man with stooped shoulders. He had bushy eyebrows and piercing gray eyes. For many years he had worked as a sand hog, digging New York tunnels.

"You mean that nice man with the whisk broom hair?" Sue said. The others laughed as they remembered Hootnanny's bristly gray hair which stood up straight on his head.

Pete took the letters up on the front porch. Holly called Pam and they all crowded around their brother as he opened the envelope addressed to the Hollister children.

"'Dear Detectives,'" the boy started to read. "'How have you all been? Did you know that I was interested in the weather? I have spent so much time working underground, that now I like to watch the sky and the clouds.

"'A very strange gadget has been found in the New York area,'" the letter continued, "'and it came by balloon from Shoreham.'"

"Maybe he found a talking parachute!" Pam interrupted.

77

Pete nodded and read on:

"'Have you children seen any balloons in the skies around your town? I think an amateur weatherman must live there. Would you please find out who he is and let me know? Now that this old sand hog has turned into a weather duck, he'd like to find a pen friend.'"

Holly chuckled when she heard this, and Pete said, "I'm not finished yet." He read on:

"'I haven't had any mysteries since you left New York and I want to see you again. Would you like to visit me?' Signed, 'Your old sand hog, Hootnanny.'"

"Would we!" Pete exclaimed as the children exchanged delighted looks.

"Mother!" Holly cried. "We've been invited to New York!"

CHAPTER 9

Red, White and Blue

THE children ran into the house to tell their mother about Hootnanny's invitation. Mrs. Hollister was in the kitchen ironing a frilly pink-and-white dress for Sue. She stood the iron on end and read the letter.

"Maybe your talking parachute mystery has reached all the way to New York," Mrs. Hollister remarked. "This is exciting."

"Please may we go?" Pete begged. "We ought to see what Hootnanny found."

"And at the same time," Pam suggested, "we could visit the American Museum of Natural History to learn more about titanium."

Mrs. Hollister handed the letter back to Pam, then ran the iron over the ruffles at the bottom of the dress. "There," she said, "that's finished," and put the frock on a hanger.

"But, Mother," Holly protested, "you haven't answered our questions."

Mrs. Hollister smiled and said, "To tell the truth, we just don't have enough money now to fly everybody to New York and back." Seeing how disappointed the children looked, she added, "Daddy and

I have a big trip planned for all of us one of these days, and we have to save up for that."

"Mother's right," Pam said. "We'll have to solve the mysteries right here in Shoreham, and we don't have any time to lose."

Pete and Pam went out to sit under a willow tree at the shore front. While they were discussing their plans, Ricky returned from his detective assignment. Hot and discouraged, he plopped down on the grass beside them, leaned on an elbow, and chewed a long stem of grass.

"No luck," he reported. "Dave and I hung around the post office but nobody came."

When Pam told him about Hootnanny's letter Ricky's face brightened. "Yikes, I remember that old codger!" he said. "Too bad we can't see him again. Pete, what'll we do about the balloons now?"

It was decided that in the afternoon Ricky and Pam should watch the sky for balloons, while Pete and Holly went to the post office to see who would come for the talking parachute in Box 48.

Having finished lunch, Pete called to Holly, and she climbed into the basket carrier of his bicycle. As Pete pedaled toward town, Pam and Ricky stretched out on the grassy lawn, gazing into the blue sky. Occasionally a fluffy cloud drifted by. Although they could see for miles around, there was not a balloon in sight.

After they had watched for nearly an hour, Ricky said, "Maybe the balloons and the parachutes come only at night. Yikes! I could be fishing."

Pam knew that she could not keep her restless brother gazing into the blue much longer. "All right, Ricky," she said, "catch a big fish for supper, and I'll—oh, look!"

She leaped to her feet and pointed to the sky over Pine Lake. Flying together high in the air were three big balloons tied together—a red, a white and a blue one. Something white dangled beneath them.

"That's a parachute!" Ricky cried. "It'll fall on Shoreham any minute!"

The balloons tumbled through the air, coming lower and lower.

"We'll follow them!" Pam declared.

She and Ricky sprang to their bicycles and rode down the street, glancing up now and then to follow the progress of the red, white and blue balloons. Still no parachute was released from them.

Up one street and down the other the two youngsters pedaled. For a few seconds they lost sight of the balloons because of the overhanging trees, but as the children broke out into the open once again, they spotted the floating objects, dropping even lower.

"Look, Ricky," Pam said, stopping her bicycle, "the balloons landed on top of that apartment house."

"Let's get them!" he replied, hopping off his bike and balancing it on the kick stand. As the two trotted toward the apartment house, Ricky saw that it was six stories high. The big front door was covered with iron grillwork, and when Ricky tried the handle he found the entrance locked.

"How are we going to get in there, Pam?" he asked. His sister suggested that they go around back. Perhaps they could find the superintendent.

"He'll help us solve the mystery when he learns we're detectives," Ricky said proudly.

The children walked along an areaway to the back of the apartment house. There, sitting in the middle of a sandbox, was a little girl, not much bigger than their sister Sue. She had blonde curly hair and large brown eyes.

"Hello, my name is Tess," the tot said, as Pam and Ricky approached. "Will you make some sand pies with me?"

"We don't have time right now. We're looking for the superintendent," Ricky told her.

"That's my Daddy," the little girl said. "I'll call him if you make sand pies with me."

"Of course we will," Pam said kindly. She sat down at the edge of the sandbox, scooped up a handful of sand, and wet it with water from a little sprinkling can which Tess gave her. Then she molded a few tiny sand pies and placed them on the edge of the sandbox to dry in the sun.

"Oh, thank you," Tess said. In a high, piping voice she called out, "Daddy! Daddy, someone's here to see you." Seconds later a dark-haired young man appeared at the basement steps. His khaki trousers were held up by suspenders and his blue work shirt was open at the neck. Pam introduced herself and told about the balloons which had landed on the roof.

"It's very important that we look at the parachute on them," Pam said, "because we have to solve a mystery."

The superintendent shook his head and said, "I'm too busy. Besides, I never let children go on the roof."

"Oh, please," Ricky pleaded, "it's important."

"Yes, Daddy," Tess piped up. "See the lovely sand pies they helped me make."

The man smiled and said, "All right, come with me. I'll take you to the roof." He led them into a cool basement where they entered an elevator and rode to the sixth floor. When they got off, Pam and Ricky followed the superintendent up a flight of stairs and onto the flat roof of the apartment house.

"There they are!" Pam said, pointing at the balloons. Ricky ran over and grabbed them just as they were about to blow off the side of the roof.

Beneath the red, white and blue balloons was a white cloth ball tied together with a tangled string. Excitedly, Pam loosened the string and down fell a banner made of cheesecloth. On it were the words, *"Bruno's three-ring Circus! Monday through Friday in Jenkintown."*

"That circus is thirty miles from here," said the

"There they are!"

man. "Too bad their banner failed to open. Is this what you were looking for?"

"No, it isn't," Pam said, crestfallen. "But thank you for helping us."

"It's what we detectives call a false clue," Ricky said. "Too bad."

The disappointed sleuths carried the balloons and the banner down in the elevator and said good-by to Tess.

"Here's something for you to play with," Pam said, handing the circus ad to the child. Tess was delighted with her gift, and skipped around the sandbox with the balloons. The Hollisters went for their bicycles and pedaled home again.

"I hope Pete and Holly had better luck than we did," Pam said as they entered the driveway.

At that very moment, her brother and sister were in the post office standing near a wall covered with private mailboxes. Now and then people came to open the small compartments and remove their letters. But nobody had come to Box Number 48.

"I feel silly just standing here watching," Holly said finally.

"I know what we can do," Pete declared. He walked over to a postal clerk and said, "I'd like six postcards, please."

"Yes sir," said the clerk, sliding the cards over the counter.

Pete paid for them and gave three to Holly. "Here," he said, "send them to somebody."

"Thanks," Holly said, as she walked to the writing desk. "Now I won't feel so conspicuous."

The children busied themselves sending postcards to Aunt Marge and Uncle Russ, their cousins, Teddy and Jean, and even to Dave Mead and Daffy. At the same time they kept an eye on Box 48, just in case the owner came for the talking parachute.

"I can't think of anybody else to write to," Holly said finally.

"Write to yourself," Pete suggested with a chuckle.

Holly was addressing the card when Joey and Will walked past the post office. Glancing inside they noticed the Hollisters.

"Psst," Joey said. "Let's see what they are doing."

The two bullies slipped quietly into the post office and stepped silently behind the girl. The black post office pen Holly was using spelled out: "Dear Holly: How are you?"

Seeing this, Joey laughed loudly, causing people to turn around and look.

"Ha, ha. Goofy Holly is sending herself a card. Tsk! Tsk! Doesn't anybody ever write to the Hollisters?"

"Don't bother us," Pete whispered hoarsely, as he saw a tall, thin man approaching Box Number 48. He turned to Holly. "Look! There he is!"

The man took a key from his pocket, opened the box, and reached his hand inside.

CHAPTER 10

Monkeyshines!

"SIR! Sir!" Pete called out. "If you don't mind, I'd like to ask you a question."

Instantly Joey and Will seized the opportunity they had been waiting for. Will snatched the cards from Holly, and Joey gave Pete a hard shove which sent him sprawling to the floor.

The bullies then fled, and by the time Pete had scrambled to his feet the tall man had vanished too.

Pete and Holly hurried outside, but all they could find were the postcards scattered on the sidewalk.

"That was the meanest trick!" Holly said indignantly.

Pete looked downcast for having lost the chance to talk with the stranger at Box 48, but he would not give up. As Pete and Holly rode their bicycles home, they decided the post office stakeout would have to continue.

"But there aren't enough of us to watch all the time," the girl protested.

"We'll call our Detective Club together," Pete replied. "Everybody can take turns staking out the post office."

"Daffy too?" Holly asked hopefully.

"Sure, she can help," Pete said. "Let's stop at her house and ask."

Pete and Holly found Daffy and her mother sewing a new dress. Mrs. Hawks invited them to have milk and cookies. While her daughter served the refreshments, Pete told of the post office episode.

When Holly asked her to help, Daffy's eyes danced. "I'd love to be one of your detectives!" she said.

"We might solve the mystery faster if we could go to New York and visit Hootnanny," Pete said, "but that's not possible." He told about the old sand hog and the letter the Hollisters had received from him.

Daffy and her mother exchanged significant glances. "Maybe the trip can be arranged," Mrs. Hawks said. "Daddy is flying to Boston with his company airplane to pick up some businessmen. He might be able to take you as far as New York."

Pete and Holly were overjoyed to hear this. Mrs. Hawks telephoned the airport and conferred with her husband. Jet Hawks said that he was leaving early the next morning and would be glad to give the Hollisters a free ride to Idlewild Airport in New York. He would call for them again the next day and return them to Shoreham.

"Yippee!" Pete exploded upon hearing the good news.

Holly jumped up and down, twirling a pigtail.

"Mother can come with us!" she cried. "Won't that be great!"

After thanking their friends, the two children pedaled home as fast as they could.

"We're all going to New York!" Pete cried as he raced into the house with Holly at his heels.

"Pete, calm down," Mrs. Hollister said. "Now tell us quietly." She broke into a big smile when she heard her son's story. "Gracious! That sounds too good to be true," she said. "I'll call Daddy and see if he can spare us for a couple of days."

The telephone call to The Trading Post brought a happy answer from Mr. Hollister. "Of course, you may all go, Elaine," he said. "A trip to New York will do you good."

The happy Hollisters' home hummed with activity that evening as the children and their mother packed their suitcases in readiness for the journey the next morning.

Pam telephoned to Hootnanny Gandy and when she told him they would land at Idlewild Airport, his voice boomed over the phone, "That's just where I'll be tomorrow morning! I'm going to visit the weather station there and watch the balloons go up." Pam made a date to meet the old sand hog at the launching site.

By the time the children were ready for bed everything had been packed for the flight the next day, and Pete had notified their playmates of the stakeout at the post office.

Shortly after daylight Mrs. Hollister awakened her family. When they had finished their breakfast the youngsters said good-by to Domingo, Zip, White Nose and her kittens. Suddenly they heard a loud meowing at the back door. There stood Casey, crying for some food.

"Mr. Kinder must still be away," Pam said as she let the tomcat into the kitchen. "I wonder what has happened to him." She spooned out a large portion of cat food, which Casey quickly ate. Then he marched to the door and took his leave with his tail in the air.

"All aboard for Jet Hawks's special to New York," Ricky called as he and Pete helped to carry the baggage into the station wagon.

Mr. Hollister drove them to the airport, where pilot Hawks had his executive jet plane ready and waiting. After good-by hugs and kisses, the family climbed aboard. When they had taken their seats beside the windows, they waved to their father.

Jet taxied the plane to the far end of the field, then headed into the wind. He gave the two engines full throttle. The craft soared off like a bird and headed toward Idlewild.

On the way Pete and Pam talked over the mysteries in which they had become involved. Mr. Kinder's disappearance had them both worried. Had he gone somewhere to sell the Castle Rock Quarry at the low figure he had been offered? Or had the old rock hound become lost on a trip to the West?

And what about the talking parachute? Was the mysterious man in Shoreham responsible for it?

"There's another mystery," Pam said, "—the monster at Castle Rock Quarry. I get the shivers when I think about that squirming thing."

"If we could only find Mr. Kinder he might be able to tell us what it was," Pete replied.

After a moment Pam said, "I hope the gadget Hootnanny found is a talking parachute. Maybe he or the weather station men will know what its purpose really is."

Sue, Holly and Ricky meanwhile had been looking down upon the patchwork quilt of farmland drifting slowly beneath the airplane. After what seemed a very short time, Jet Hawks announced that he was descending, and minutes later the plane touched down at Idlewild.

The pilot lowered a ramp from the back of the airplane and the family stepped out, carrying their luggage.

"I must take off soon again and head for Boston," the flyer told them. "Meet me here at ten o'clock tomorrow night." Then he went back into his airplane and prepared to set off.

As the Hollisters walked toward the terminal building a small hand truck zoomed past piled high with crates.

"Look," said Pete, "there must be animals in those boxes. See the wire screen fronts."

The vehicle swerved around a baggage truck and

one of the crates toppled off. *Smash!* The wooden slats broke open and out hopped a small kangaroo.

The creature stood blinking in the sunlight, as the truck went on without stopping.

"Oh!" was all the Hollisters could say for a moment. Then everyone talked at once.

"Come back!" Ricky shouted, running after the unheeding truck. "You lost something!"

"We've got to catch the kangaroo," said Pete, "before he gets hurt." As the children rushed toward the animal, it took a few unsteady leaps away from the broken crate.

"Stop, stop!" cried Pam. The children cautiously encircled the kangaroo. Then Pete firmly picked it up in his arms.

"Good work, son!" said a passing pilot, and there was a smattering of applause from several airline attendants who had witnessed the capture.

"What'll I do with it?" Pete asked.

"Take it to the animal shelter at the far end of the airport," an attendant suggested. "It's near the weather station."

"That's just where we're going," Pam said.

"It's a long walk," the attendant added smiling. "Wait now, here's a pickup truck going your way. Why don't you all pile in?"

The man hailed the driver who stopped the vehicle. Eying the kangaroo, he grinned. "I haven't room for all of you," he said.

Mrs. Hollister volunteered to wait in the termi-

"Good work, son," said the passing pilot.

nal building with Sue. She instructed the children where to meet her, adding, "Don't be longer than an hour."

Holly and Ricky hopped up into the cab, while Pete and Pam climbed on the rear. The kangaroo wiggled and kicked.

"Whew! I hope we get there fast," Pete said.

The animal shelter was a brick structure several miles from the arrivals building. When they pulled up in front of it, a stocky man with a broad smiling face strode toward them.

"Tim," he called to the driver, "I see you've found the runaway kangaroo."

"Credit these young 'uns," Tim replied. "They caught him."

Pete handed the animal to the man, who said, "Follow me, children." He led them into the building and down a long corridor to a room with rows of cages in it. He carefully put the kangaroo in one of these.

"Now," he said, turning to the Hollisters. "My name is Mr. Moody. I'm in charge of this place. It's a sort of hotel for animals waiting to be picked up or sent out of the airport."

Pete introduced himself and the others and explained how they had found the kangaroo. While he talked, the Hollisters heard a chattering noise.

"Monkeys," Mr. Moody said smiling. "One hundred crates of them." He explained that the monkeys had come from overseas and were being sent to laboratories and zoos.

"One box contains a circus monkey," Mr. Moody said. "Red Hat—that's his name—is the smartest one of the lot."

"May we see them?" Ricky asked.

"Sure." Mr. Moody led them back into the corridor and through another door.

What a chatter the monkeys made as the children walked into the room! Cage was piled on top of cage, reaching nearly to the ceiling.

"We've handled everything from anteaters to elephants," the animal man said.

"And lions too?" Holly asked, wide-eyed.

"Lions too, and baby gorillas," came the reply.

Mr. Moody excused himself to get a dish of cool water and some food for the kangaroo. While he was gone the children went close to the monkey cages.

"Oh look," Ricky said. "I think this is the circus monkey." He peered into a cage, the door of which was held tight by a simple nail catch.

"Oh! Isn't he cute," Pam exclaimed. "What a funny little hat and red vest he's wearing!"

"Hello, Red Hat!" Holly said.

The monkey chattered, doffed his cap, and bobbed his head toward the children.

While Pete, Pam and Ricky moved on to other cages, Holly stood fascinated by Red Hat. She removed the nail and stuck it playfully through the

95

wire mesh of the little screen door. Quick as a wink, Red Hat's skinny brown hand grabbed the nail away from her.

"Please give it back," Holly said. But the little monkey only jabbered and tipped his hat.

"Come on," Pete called from the door. "We have to go now. Hootnanny's expecting us."

"But, but—" Holly said, lingering at Red Hat's cage.

"We must hurry," Pam said, taking her sister by the hand. The children left the big room and closed the door behind them.

Mr. Moody met them in the corridor, and as they said good-by the chatter of the monkeys grew louder and louder.

"Something's going wrong in there," the custodian said, frowning. He went to the door, stepped inside, and cried out in dismay. The monkeys were out of their cages and climbing all over the place!

CHAPTER 11

The Radar Clue

"COME in quickly!" exclaimed Mr. Moody, "and shut the door!"

The children slipped into the room behind him and Ricky exclaimed, "Yikes!"

Monkeys swarmed all over the place. Freed from their cages, they swung, leaped and chattered.

Red Hat seemed to be having the most fun of all, as he opened another cage and six more of his companions leaped to freedom.

"So you're the guilty one!" Mr. Moody said, grabbing for Red Hat. "I'll put you back in the cage first, you rascal." But the monkey slipped out of his grasp, tipped his hat, and gave a toothy grin.

Holly tugged the custodian's hand and looked up at him with a sorrowful face. "Put me in a cage, Mr. Moody," she said. "I'm the real rascal, not poor Red Hat."

"Holly! What are you saying?" Pam declared above the din. The little girl told them about the latch and looked more crestfallen than ever.

"What's done is done," Mr. Moody said. "We must move quickly before Red Hat frees more of his friends. He hurried to a closet, pulled out three long-handled nets, and handed one each to Pete and Pam. "Quick," he ordered. "Red Hat first!"

The three nets swished this way and that, but the agile circus monkey ducked away each time.

"We'll never catch him," Ricky moaned. "He's too full of wiggles."

"Wait," Mr. Moody said. He went to a cabinet and returned with a banana, which he put in Pete's hand. "Now you'll see how curiosity can catch a monkey."

The custodian pulled a handkerchief from his pocket. With a flick of the wrist he opened the white square and draped it over the fruit.

"Stand quietly and watch," Mr. Moody said. The Hollisters obeyed.

In a few seconds Red Hat swung down from the top of the cages and landed on a crate beside Pete. Then the monkey cautiously reached out to lift the handkerchief.

"Get him, Pam," Mr. Moody whispered, and the girl swished her net over the monkey's head.

"Hurray, you caught him," Holly cried gleefully.

Grasping the prisoner firmly, Mr. Moody took Red Hat out of the net and locked him securely in his cage.

"Now that we have the ringleader of the monkey-shines," he said, "the rest will be easier to catch. I can manage it alone." He thanked the children for helping him, and gave Holly a big wink as they left the shelter.

Pete led the youngsters to the weather station, where the Hollisters were to meet Hootnanny.

The building, a short distance away, was easy to identify. It was made of concrete and had no windows. One wall of the building was open, and inside three men were guiding a huge balloon out of it, while a tall man watched.

"Hootnanny!" Holly cried and raced ahead to her old friend, her pigtails blowing in the wind.

At that instant the crew let go the balloon, and it rose into the sky. Hootnanny caught Holly up in his arms and shouted, "There she goes! A perfect take-off!"

As the big balloon soared, an orange parachute swung below it on strings. Under the chute hung a square instrument box. The Hollisters and Hootnanny watched the big sphere rise and grow smaller in the sky.

"I'm glad you got here in time to see the train go," Hootnanny said, greeting each of the children.

"What train?" Pete asked.

"That's what we weathermen call the balloon, the parachute and the instrument box all together," the old man explained. "It's short for instrument train."

"You tell 'em, Hootnanny!" called out one of the crewmen, a young fellow with dark curly hair. "Are these the detectives you were telling us about?"

"None other," the old sand hog replied proudly

"A perfect take-off," said Hootnanny.

as the man walked over to them. "Harry Freeman, I'd like you to meet the Happy Hollisters."

As they shook hands Hootnanny continued, "Mr. Freeman's in charge of launching the weather balloons."

"Show the children what you found," the young man said.

Hootnanny reached into his pocket and pulled out a small object.

"Why, that's part of a talking parachute!" Pam exclaimed.

"It talked, all right," Hootnanny replied. "How did you know?"

"We found one just like it," Pete said excitedly. "What does this one say?"

"The record is scratched," the old man replied. "All we can make out is 'Send me to—Shoreham.'"

"Post Office Box 48," the children chorused. Quickly Pete told the two men how he and Pam had found the talking parachute and sent it to the post office.

"We've got the members of our Detective Club watching there now," Pam explained. "We're almost sure to catch the person who comes after it."

The two men exchanged smiles. Hootnanny shook his head. "How do you like that? I ask them to come to help us, and they've got the case half solved before they get here!"

"The talking parachute is a very useful invention," Mr. Freeman told them. "The Weather Bureau likes to have their instrument packets returned after they fall to earth. They can usually be repaired and used again."

"And the lights on the parachute and the talk-box make it easy to find," Hootnanny added. "It's a dandy gizmo!"

"We'd like to get in touch with the inventor. Maybe he would sell it to us," Mr. Freeman concluded.

The children promised to keep trying to find the man.

"Where is your mother?" Hootnanny boomed suddenly. "You didn't come alone!" Pam told him where Mrs. Hollister was waiting with Sue.

"It's nearly noon," the young weatherman put in. "I'm going that way. I'll take you in my car."

A short time later Hootnanny and the four children joined Sue and Mrs. Hollister at the air terminal, where they all had a jolly lunch together. Then they took a bus into New York and went directly to a large hotel next to Central Park.

After Mrs. Hollister had registered, she said, "We have shopping to do this afternoon, children. The girls need new dresses."

Pam and Holly hugged each other, and Sue clapped her hands. Pete and Ricky looked disappointed.

"Men don't care a hootnanny about shoppin'," the sand hog said. "How about the boys and me takin' a trip together? Reckon I got somethin' special to show 'em."

"Have a good time," Mrs. Hollister said, smiling. "See you later."

Pete hailed a taxicab and soon they were at Rockefeller Center. Hootnanny led them into a tall building and up one flight of stairs to an open mezzanine hallway.

"Here's the Weather Bureau," he said, opening a door. "They all know me here." The boys went inside to see a room full of desks and charts and weathermen busy at their work.

"Hello, Mr. Pogue," Hootnanny said, approaching one of the men. "I have some visitors here with news for you."

Mr. Pogue was a short, stocky, brisk-moving man with a full mustache. The old sand hog introduced the boys to him and told how they were on the trail of the talking-parachute man.

"That's fine, boys," Mr. Pogue said. "We'd certainly like to find the fellow who sends up these gadgets."

"Speakin' of gizmos," said Hootnanny, "I'd like to show them the radarscope."

Mr. Pogue smiled. "Follow me." He led them to a door which he opened quietly. Inside it was pitch dark except for a dim, glowing light on an instrument panel.

As everyone's eyes grew accustomed to the darkness Pete and Ricky saw that a man sat before a whole bank of instruments, in the middle of which was the circular radarscope. A long finger of light flicked round and round.

"The engineer will tell you how it works," Mr. Pogue said. The operator pointed to tiny black areas showing on the radarscope.

"Those are rain clouds," he explained. "By their position we can tell that it's raining in Connecticut and in western New Jersey."

"Can you see airplanes and things?" Ricky asked.

"Yes," the man replied, "also ships coming into the harbor."

"Balloons, too?" said Pete. He told of the talking parachute which they had discovered in Shoreham.

"Occasionally I pick up strange objects on the 'scope in your area. We think they're weather balloons, but not ours."

"I'll bet they're what the talk-boxes were dropped from," Pete said.

Mr. Pogue thought so, too, and encouraged the boys in their sleuthing. Then he said, "Would you like to see our weather station in Central Park?"

"Crickets! That's keen!" Pete exclaimed.

They thanked the radar operator and left the Weather Bureau office with Hootnanny and Mr. Pogue.

Outside the building was parked a government station wagon. Mr. Pogue took the wheel and drove north through heavy traffic into Central Park. After winding along the road for a way, Mr. Pogue turned onto a path which took them to a small lake. On the shore of it was a rocky hill on top of which stood a small castle.

"This is Belvedere Tower," Hootnanny said as they all got out. He pointed to the turret where there were two weather vanes with cups on the ends of the crossarms. "Anemometers," Hootnanny told the boys. "One tells the speed of the wind, the other how hard it blows."

Mr. Pogue took a key from his pocket, opened the door, and led the children up a narrow winding stairway to the top of the weather station.

"What a wonderful view of Central Park!" Pete exclaimed.

"You can go still higher," the weatherman said, motioning the brothers to a steep spiral stairway. Pete and Ricky scrambled to the top of the tower, climbed out on the turret, and looked about.

"Yikes! I can see all of Manhattan," Ricky said.

"And to think the Indians sold it for a handful of trinkets!" Pete said, surveying the towering skyline.

Springing like a mountain goat, Ricky stood daringly on the very top of the turret.

"You'd better get off," Pete cautioned him. But as Ricky hopped down, his foot slipped on the smooth granite.

CHAPTER 12

The Big Museum

As Ricky dropped, he grabbed the edge of the turret with his fingers. Pete reached over and seized his brother's belt. "Help! Mr. Pogue!" he shouted.

The weatherman ran up the spiral stairs, with Hootnanny at his heels. Seeing Ricky dangling, the men pulled the boy to safety.

"Whew!" said Mr. Pogue, as Hootnanny wiped his brow.

Much subdued, the brothers followed the grown-ups downstairs and outside. "I'm sorry," Ricky said ruefully when they were seated in the Weather Bureau car again.

"It just ain't safe in high places," Hootnanny said shaking his finger. "Now, tunnels, that's the safest place of all!"

On the return drive through Central Park Mr. Pogue stopped at a vendor's cart and bought four ice cream bars. "I think we could all use a little pick-me-up," he declared.

When they arrived at the hotel the boys and Hootnanny thanked Mr. Pogue and said good-by.

"Good luck on your detective work," the weatherman said. "Keep it up. We need your help."

The girls and Mrs. Hollister already had returned from their shopping trip with several of the latest-style frocks. They excitedly listened to the boys' report about the radar clue, then made plans for the next day.

"I want to see the mineral man at the museum," Pam said, "to ask some more questions about titanium."

"Good," Mrs. Hollister said. "We'll all go to the museum; and will we see you later, Hootnanny?"

"Of course," Hootnanny said, raising his eyebrows in a surprised look. "You're havin' dinner with me at my home."

Sue giggled. "Oh, you can't cook, Hootnanny. You're a sand piggy."

"Oh ho! Well, I'll surprise you with my cooking. And not only that, I have another surprise for you, too."

"What is it, please?" Holly begged.

"It's a bird, that's all I'll say," Hootnanny replied. "Well, good-by. Dinner's at seven!"

"What's old Hooty up to now?" Pete said with a grin after their friend had left.

"We'll learn that tomorrow," Pam remarked. "Don't be impatient, Pete."

Next day the Hollisters arrived at the American Museum of Natural History before noon. They stood on the sidewalk and looked up at the big building, which covered several blocks. As they trooped up the wide steps to the front door Sue asked, "What's in here?"

"Animals in glass cases," Ricky replied, taking two steps at a time.

The Hollisters entered the museum and found themselves in a large marble hall with a high dome.

"Crickets!" Pete said. "It's big, all right!"

"Yes," Mrs. Hollister agreed. "We'd better stay together, so no one gets lost." As she spoke, Sue pointed into the dimly lit hall to their left. In the middle of the floor loomed three enormous elephants.

"Are they real?" asked Sue.

"They were alive once," Mrs. Hollister said, "but now they're stuffed and mounted."

"Everything in here is stuffed," Ricky said importantly. "See?" He pointed to the lighted glass windows on either side of the darkened hall. In each were animals which looked alive, posed amongst their native surroundings.

"Here's a scary one!" Holly called from down the corridor. The others joined her to stare through the glass at a tiger prowling through a dark, snow-covered forest.

"I thought tigers lived in hot jungles," Ricky commented.

"Not all of them," Pete replied, reading the sign beside the cage. "This is a Siberian tiger."

"Listen!" Pam said. "I hear birds." The soft

"Are they real?" asked Sue.

twittering and shrill cries seemed to come from nearby.

"Let's find them," Holly said. She skipped around a corner, and suddenly spied a red-skinned man standing in a jungle grove. He had a large bow, and was aiming an arrow into the sky. Real-looking vines hung down from the trees and sunlight filtered through the heavy leaves. The strange bird cries seemed to come right from the jungle around the hunter.

"Those must be recorded calls," Pete said.

"It's a Montaña Indian from South America," Pam explained, reading the sign.

The other children moved on and Mrs. Hollister took Sue's hand. The little girl was staring hard at the statue of the Indian and frowning. As she walked away with her mother, she looked back once.

Pete led the others down a wide staircase and turned right into an enormous, well-lighted hall. In the middle of it was a huge Indian canoe. Excitedly the children hurried over to the odd craft.

"That's a thousand times bigger than any canoe I ever saw!" Ricky exclaimed. In it sat life-sized, dark-skinned rowers dressed in furry hides. At each end stood a man wearing an animal-skin robe and a grotesque totem mask on his head.

Again Sue looked troubled, and called out in a loud voice, "Mummy, where did all the stuffed people come from?"

"They're not real people," Mrs. Hollister explained, "and they never were. They're just big, big dolls."

"But they don't look like Maddie-Poo."

"That's 'cause they're old Indians," Holly put in.

The giant canoe fascinated Holly, and she lingered to gaze at the stern-faced figures. Glancing about, she edged close to the side of the craft, but the guard motioned her away.

"Come on," Ricky said, taking Holly's hand. "There's more to see!" He led his sister into a corridor and all at once faced two wolves who raced across the moonlit snow directly toward them, their eyes glittering hungrily.

"Yikes," he muttered. "I'm glad they're stuffed."

Holly giggled. "But I'm not stuffed. I feel empty."

"I'm hungry, too," Ricky said, and when his mother came along he suggested lunch.

"I could eat a lion," Mrs. Hollister said with a twinkle in her eyes, "but I think I'll have a sandwich instead."

They made their way to the museum cafeteria and had a tasty snack. As they finished dessert of pink and white sherbet, Pete said, "Now to the mineral hall. We might find another good clue to the quarry mystery."

The Hollisters went into the corridor and stood with a large crowd waiting for the elevator. When the door opened, they stepped inside the lift, and Pete asked for the mineral hall.

"Third floor," replied the operator, as the elevator started up.

"Here we are," Mrs. Hollister declared a moment later, leading her brood. "Come everybody."

The Hollisters entered the Mineral Hall, and while the others looked in the glass cases at big chunks of colorful and sparkling rocks, Pam asked a guard where they could find the Chairman of the Department of Mineralogy.

"He's not here today," replied the guard, "but you could talk to his assistant. He's in his office." The guard pointed out into the corridor.

Pam thanked him and returned to tell the others.

"Sue and I will wait for you on the bench at the elevators," Mrs. Hollister said.

The children walked to the office door and knocked. "Come in," said a voice. As they entered, a young man in shirt sleeves swiveled around and looked surprised. "What can I do for you?" he asked, removing his dark-rimmed glasses. Quickly Pete showed him the piece of stone with the gold threads in it.

"Hmm, titanium," the assistant said.

"We'd like to know if there would be a lot of it in a quarry near our town," Pete explained.

The young man led them to a large map. "Show me where you live," he said. Pete searched a moment, then pointed to Shoreham.

"The answer to your question is yes," said the young mineralogist. "Titanium can be found in your section of the country. There may be a vein of it in your quarry."

The children exclaimed in excitement. The assistant smiled. "If you find the titanium what'll you do with it?" he asked, his eyes twinkling. "Make diamonds?"

The children looked puzzled. "What do you mean?" Pam asked.

"Scientists know how to make artificial diamonds from this mineral," the man replied. "They are very beautiful, but, of course, they are not as hard or expensive as the real ones."

Pete grinned. "First we'll have to find the vein in the quarry."

"Well, I wish you luck!" said the assistant. The children thanked him and left the office, bubbling with excitement. When they reached their mother they all began to talk at once.

"Wait—wait!" protested Mrs. Hollister, looking over her children. "Where is Holly?" The others glanced around, then at each other. No one knew.

"Yikes!" said Ricky, thinking of the miles of dark corridors.

Sue's eyes filled with tears. "Holly's lost," she quavered.

CHAPTER 13

A Spotted Owl

"DON'T cry, Sue," said Pam. "We'll find Holly."

"Maybe the guard in the Mineral Hall saw her," Pete suggested. "Let's ask him."

The Hollisters hurried down the corridor and into the big room with the glass cases. The guard was looking into one of the exhibits when the family approached him.

"Excuse me," Mrs. Hollister said quickly. "Have you seen a little girl with pigtails? My daughter, Holly Hollister, is missing."

The man's blue eyes were sympathetic, but he did not seem surprised. "No, I can't say I have," he replied. "When was the last time you saw her?"

"She was behind me when we got on the elevator," Ricky said. No one could recall seeing her after that.

The guard sighed and shook his head. "She could be anywhere. It's a mighty big building!"

"We'd better divide up and start hunting for her," Pete said anxiously.

"Not so fast, young fellow," the guard replied. "There's a quicker way. I'll have an announcement made on the public address system. Holly will hear that wherever she is. Where do you want to meet her?"

"At the front door," Mrs. Hollister said, "and thank you so much."

In two minutes the loud-speakers throughout the museum broadcast the message:

"Holly Hollister, please meet your mother at the front door." This was repeated several times, but Holly failed to appear.

Twenty minutes later, as the family waited anxiously at the front door, there was still no sign of the missing girl.

"Something must have happened to her," Pete said, worried. Pam thought hard. One of the things Holly had been most interested in was the big Indian canoe.

"Mother," Pam said, "maybe she went back to the hall downstairs. Pete and I had better go look."

"All right," replied Mrs. Hollister. "The rest of us will wait here in case she comes."

Pete and Pam ran through the dim corridors, down the stairs, and into the big hall. A guard stood beside the canoe as spectators moved around it. Holly was nowhere to be seen.

"Oh dear, where can she be!" Pam said, and then, ignoring the crowd of people, she called out, "Holly, please come, wherever you are!"

The startled onlookers turned to stare at Pam, and as they did so two eyes peeked over the edge of the war canoe.

Pete was first to spy them. "Crickets!" he exclaimed, recognizing his sister. "Holly's in the canoe!"

The little girl's head ducked out of sight, but the guard had seen her, too. He hastened over and pulled her out of the ancient craft.

"Holly Hollister!" Pam cried. "What were you doing in there?"

"When the guard wasn't looking I—I climbed up to look at the funny stuffed Indians—and fell in," Holly said. "Then I was afraid to get out."

"Tsk, tsk," the guard said, shaking his head. "Take her to her mother."

"I'm sorry!" Holly burst out in tears and flung her arms around Pam.

"Now, now!" the guard said, patting her head. "Turn off the waterworks! I'll tell the office you've been found."

Pete and Pam thanked the guard for his help and they hurried away with Holly between them.

When Mrs. Hollister saw her missing daughter she hugged her, and Holly poured out the story again.

"I ought to scold you," Mrs. Hollister said, "but I'm so glad to have you back that I won't."

As they left the museum, Sue slipped her hand in Holly's and the pigtailed girl dried her eyes.

"Yikes!" Ricky said. "Didn't we have a keen time!"

That evening, promptly at seven, the Hollisters'

"*Crickets, it's Holly!*"

taxi drew up in front of a neat-looking apartment building in Greenwich Village. While his mother paid the driver, Pete pushed the buzzer. A moment later Hootnanny welcomed them into his ground-floor apartment.

The living room was just as the children remembered it, neat and plain, but now there was a round table in the center covered with a red-checked cloth. It was set for seven people.

"Crickets! Look at this!" Pete exclaimed going over to a large map which covered part of one wall.

"Reckon I keep up with the weather fronts on that," Hootnanny said, stepping into his alcove kitchen. He tied on an apron and lifted the lid from a big black pot. A delicious aroma wafted out into the room as he filled seven bowls with hearty-looking stew.

The girls helped carry the dishes to the table, and in a twinkling Hootnanny had salad, bread and milk there, too.

"Sit down now," he invited and grinned. "Surprised to learn I can cook? When we're done eatin', I'll show you a better surprise than that!"

After they had finished the delicious dinner everyone helped with the dishes.

As Sue put the last fork away, Hootnanny said, "Now, young Hollisters, shut your eyes and face the table." The children obeyed, smiling, and a moment later the old man ordered, "Open!"

Standing on the table was a large cutout of a blue owl!

"It's a present for you," Hootnanny said. "This owl has a secret. See if you can figure it out."

The children gathered eagerly around as Pam picked up the big-eyed bird and looked it over. "It's made of blotting paper," she said.

"With a cardboard back and stand," Pete added.

"And the eyes and wings are black paper pasted on the blotter," Holly observed.

"Oh, it's so cute," Sue said. "Does it hoot, Hootnanny?"

The old sand hog shook his head no, but said, "I'll give you a hint. This owl's name is Weather Wise."

Pete suddenly grinned. "I know the secret!" he exclaimed. "But I won't give it away."

"Oh, I know, too," Pam said. "Blue is the clue!"

Ricky and Holly and Sue puzzled over the owl.

"I'm awfully thirsty," Sue said. "May I have a drink of water, please?"

"Help yourself," the old man said. "There's a glass on the sink."

"I want one, too," Ricky said and followed Sue. He was still holding the owl.

The girl reached up on tiptoes and turned the faucet on, full force. The water shot out with such a rush that it splashed all over the sink.

"Watch out!" Ricky cried and jumped back. But

too late. The blue owl was covered with drops of water. Sue's eyes grew wide as she saw the spots turning pink in color.

"Yikes!" cried Ricky. "You've spoiled the present!"

As Sue and Ricky turned from the sink, they were surprised to see that Pete, Pam and Hootnanny were grinning.

"You haven't spoiled the owl," Pam said. "It's supposed to turn pink when it gets wet. That's the secret."

"Whenever it's going to rain," Hootnanny told them, "there's lots of moisture in the air. The blotting paper soaks it up and turns pink. That tells you it's likely to rain."

"When the air is dry the owl becomes blue again," Pam added.

The three younger children did not quite understand. "Is the blue paint magic?" Sue asked.

"No," Pete said. "The owl is painted with a chemical called cobalt chloride. We did an experiment with it in school and I showed Pam. That's how we knew the secret."

"I'm so glad Weather Wise isn't hurt," Ricky said happily setting the owl on the table.

"I wish we had one for Daffy," Pam said.

"They're easy to make," Hootnanny told her. "I'll give you some cobalt." He went quickly to the kitchen, took a small bottle from a top shelf, and handed it to Pam. "There now," he declared, "that's enough to make a whole zoo, but don't forget you've got a mystery man to trace."

"And now we have an airplane to catch," Mrs. Hollister added with a smile. "Jet expects us at ten o'clock."

They thanked Hootnanny warmly for his party and his gifts, and promised to keep in touch.

When the Hollisters met Jet at the airport, the spots on the owl were almost dry, and by the time they landed at Shoreham, Weather Wise was his old blue self again.

Jet Hawks's station wagon was parked at the airport and he drove the Hollisters home.

"It was a wonderful trip," Mrs. Hollister said and thanked Jet Hawks for his kindness.

The pilot grinned, gave the whole family a snappy salute, and set off for his own home.

"By the way, Pete," Mr. Hollister said, as the children prepared for bed, "Dave Mead has been telephoning for you all evening."

"Did he leave a message, Dad?"

"Yes. A very brief one, and very mysterious, too."

"About the stakeout at the post office?"

"I don't know," Mr. Hollister replied. "All he said was, 'Tell Pete to call me in the morning. I have big news.'"

CHAPTER 14

Domingo & Co.

PETE went to sleep thinking about Dave's message. He was awakened by a hand shaking his shoulder, and looked up sleepily into the face of Dave himself.

"Get up, lazy bones," his friend said.

Pete sat upright and rubbed his eyes. "What time is it?" he asked.

"Eight o'clock. But I had to see you early. We found the man who comes to Post Office Box 48!"

"Crickets! That's great, Dave." Pete bounded out of bed and dressed hurriedly. "How did you find him?"

"The stakeout worked. Ann Hunter saw him come for a letter."

Hearing the exclamations of the two boys, Pam knocked on the door and entered as Pete slipped into his shoes.

"You've found the man!" she whispered excitedly. "What's his name?"

"Karl Anthony," Dave replied. "He was in a hurry and couldn't stop to chat with Ann but he gave her his address."

"Then we'll see him right away," Pete said. He

and Pam ate breakfast, and the three left quietly so as not to awaken the other children. They rode their bicycles to the far side of town and knocked on the door of the bungalow where Mr. Anthony lived. The man was just about to leave for work, but on seeing the children he ushered them in.

Pete noticed instantly that this was the same person whom he and Holly had seen in the post office. After introductions Mr. Anthony said, "Hollister. Oh yes, there was postcard from you in Box 48. Why do you want to get in touch with the owner?"

Pete explained their interest in the talking parachute.

"Oh that," Mr. Anthony said. "Well, I'm acting for a friend. He's an inventor. Name's Link."

"When will you see him again?" Pete asked.

"I don't know. Link comes here every Friday night to pick up his mail and the gadgets which have been sent back, but he didn't come last week."

"Do you know where he is?" Pam asked.

"I wish I did," Mr. Anthony said, worriedly. "There was an article in yesterday's *Eagle* asking him to come forward, and now you have news for him, too. It's not like him to go off without telling me."

Mr. Anthony said that his friend was conducting experiments somewhere outside of town. "He lives there during the week, but I don't know where it is."

"Today's Friday," Pete said. "If he comes to-night will you have him get in touch with us? His invention may prove very valuable to the weather bureau."

Mr. Anthony said he would do this, and the children left.

On the way back Pete and Pam stopped at Mr. Kinder's house, but Dave had to go on home. The old rock hound's place was deserted. Pete and Pam queried several neighbors but they did not know where the old fellow had gone.

"It's odd," said a stout little woman who lived across the street. "He never leaves Casey. Why, I'm feeding that cat all the time."

"So are we," Pete said with a chuckle. "What an appetite!"

The children went back to Mr. Kinder's house and left a note under the door asking him to get in touch with them.

"It sure is queer," Pete mused. "The two men we need to find are *both* missing."

"Yes," Pam agreed. "And we have no clue at all to where Mr. Link is."

"Mr. Kinder might be staying at the quarry for some reason," Pete said, "and we just haven't seen him."

Pam suggested an overnight trip to Castle Rock. "We can look for Mr. Kinder and prospect for titanium at the same time."

"And maybe solve the mystery of the monster,"

Pete added. Excited with the idea, they cycled swiftly home.

At lunch time Mr. Hollister agreed that Indy Roades might escort them on an overnight quarry trip, and when Pam telephoned the Indian at The Trading Post, he readily agreed.

"Let's take Domingo," the man suggested. "We can pack supplies on the donkey in our tour around the quarry."

"Good!" Pam replied. "Perhaps he can carry the sacks of titanium ore if we find any."

When they had finished eating, Pam called Daffy to invite her to go to the quarry with them. "I wish I could," said the girl, "but Daddy is taking us on a two-day trip tomorrow."

"Oh, I'm sorry," Pam said, "but I'll tell you all about it when we return."

After the girls had said good-by, Pete telephoned Mr. Kent and told him about Hootnanny's talking parachute and the visit to Mr. Anthony.

"Now all you have to do is wait for the inventor to pick up his mail tonight," Mr. Kent said jovially. "And you'll have caught your man."

"I just hope Link comes," Pete said to himself after the editor had hung up.

For the rest of the day Pete and Pam, Holly and Ricky prepared for the big adventure at Castle Rock.

Sue agreed with her mother that it might be more fun for her to stay at home and make a spe-

Pete led Domingo up the ramp.

cial new set of doll clothes to await Maddie-Poo on her return from the doll hospital. Even Domingo seemed excited as Holly and Ricky currycombed him for the safari.

Pete's eagerness, however, was dimmed somewhat by the telephone call he made to Mr. Anthony. The man reported that Mr. Link still was among the missing.

"If I don't hear from him soon," Mr. Anthony said, "I shall notify the police."

Next morning Indy arrived early, driving a truck with stake sides. A ramp was lowered from the back, and Pete led Domingo up into the vehicle. After he tied the burro securely, Pam, Ricky and Holly helped to carry sleeping bags, food supplies and a small camp stove into the truck.

Before they set off, Ricky raced into the house and returned with his father's battered old fishing hat. "If I'm going to be a prospector," he said with a grin, "I'd better look like one!"

The brothers climbed into the back of the truck with Domingo while the girls sat alongside Indy.

"Good-by, good-by!" they shouted as the truck started off toward Castle Rock quarry. Mrs. Hollister and Sue waved from the driveway.

"Eee-aw, ee-aw!" brayed Domingo.

An hour later the young adventurers were bouncing over the rough road which led into the quarry. Finally the huge pit yawned before them, silent and hot in the bright morning sunshine. Indy drove into the quarry and toward the pond.

One of the boats was tied up at the edge of the water. The other floated in the middle with a fisherman seated in it. A straw hat was pulled low over his face, but Pete recognized him as Sid Raff. The man glanced up at the Hollisters but paid no more attention than that.

As they drove along the bottom of the vast rocky cut, Pete pointed to what he thought would be a good place for them to set up camp. It was at the base of the cliff in a cove sheltered from the wind.

When the truck stopped, the children alighted, let down the tail gate, and unloaded Domingo. Then the rest of the gear, including ropes and child-size pickaxes, was taken out.

As Pete and Pam dragged the tents to a level spot, the boy glanced up at the rim of the quarry. Near one of the turrets of Castle Rock, Pete noticed an old dead pine tree standing precariously at the very edge of the cliff.

While the others pitched camp, Ricky and Holly dashed up to the pond and hallooed to Sid Raff.

"We're prospectors!" Ricky cried out, waving.

"So I can see," the man called back. "Good luck to you."

"Have you seen Mr. Kinder?" Holly shouted.

The man shook his head no and continued fishing.

Once the tent had been set up and the stores

put in their proper place, Pam opened the sandwich lunch Mrs. Hollister had provided. After they had eaten, Pete suggested they go prospecting immediately.

The children flung several empty sacks over Domingo's back, and taking picks and shovels they set off with Indy. Several minutes later they started up the steep path which led to the rim of the quarry.

Glancing back, Pete and Pam saw Raff beaching his boat, but when they looked again a few moments later, the man had disappeared.

"Crickets," Pete said, "he's done it again!"

"Where could he have gone so fast?" Pam asked.

The others scanned the empty sun-baked quarry. There was no sign of the fisherman.

"He must have a secret hiding place in the cliff wall," Pete said. "Maybe a cave."

"If Sid Raff knows of one," Pam suggested, "Mr. Kinder might, too. Perhaps that's where he is."

"We'll search for caves before we leave," Pete agreed.

The young prospectors moved on slowly, examining pieces of rock here and there and digging out specimens as they went along.

"Oh look!" Pam exclaimed, pointing to a large chunk sticking from the face of the cliff some distance from the path. She reached forward with her pick, but it was too far away.

"Pete, will you hold my hand, please," Pam

asked. When her brother did this, Pam leaned far to one side and swung her pick at the jutting rock.

The force, however, made her moist hand slip from Pete's grip.

"Oh!" Pam gasped. The pick hit the stone a solid whack and it popped from the rock wall. Then Pam, the stone and a shower of gravel tumbled down the slope. Amid a haze of dust Pam finally came to a stop against a large boulder. Her face was smudged and she had several scratches on her arms. Pete and Indy were at her side in seconds.

"Pam! Are you hurt?" Pete shouted.

"I'm all right," she replied, "but I guess I'm not a very good prospector."

Ricky ran back to camp and returned with a small first-aid kit which Mrs. Hollister had put in a knapsack. Indy quickly painted her scratches and Holly remarked, "Pam, you look like an Indian on the warpath."

Ricky meanwhile gathered up the fallen gravel in one of the bags and when he had finished he and Pete heaved it on Domingo's back.

"Let's go back to the pond and wash the stones clean," Holly suggested.

While the two girls took Domingo and did this, the boys and Indy explored the rock walls below the castle formation and on either side of it. Because this was the oldest part of the quarry, the cliffs were heavily overgrown with brush. The searchers found no cave or opening into which Sid Raff could have disappeared.

"That doesn't mean there isn't one," Pete said. "We could easily have missed it."

When the boys and Indy returned to camp they found the girls preparing for supper.

"We washed about a million stones," Holly reported, "but none of them had gold threads in them. Did you find a secret passage?"

Pete shook his head. "What are you making?" he asked.

"Pigs in blankets," Holly replied.

"Yikes, that's great!" Ricky said and gathered long green sticks while Pete and Indy started the fire. Meanwhile each girl poured prepared biscuit mix into an empty coffee can and added canned milk to make dough. Pam then speared wieners on the sticks Ricky had gathered and Holly wrapped a dough "blanket" around the middle of each "pig."

The hungry prospectors roasted these over the hot coals and drank milk which had been kept cool in their small portable icebox.

"What's for dessert?" asked Ricky.

"Angels on horseback," Holly replied. "I'll show you how to fix your own." She placed four thin squares of chocolate on a graham cracker. "That's the horse," she explained, "and here's the angel." She plopped a hot toasted marshmallow onto it and covered it with a graham cracker lid. Ricky bit into the sandwich and rolled his eyes.

"Mmm," he said.

It was dusk by the time they had cleaned up. When it was dark Pete doused the fire.

"Why did you do that?" Ricky asked. "I wanted to roast some more marshmallows after a while."

"It's better to watch the quarry in the dark," the older boy explained. "If that monster shows his head again we can see it without being seen."

For over an hour the campers sat quietly scanning the huge dark pit around them. Suddenly Pam pointed high into the air and the others looked up. A small bonfire flickered near Castle Rock. As the children watched, it began to turn green.

"Yikes!" Ricky exclaimed. "Maybe that's the monster and he's breathing green fire!"

"Let's get a closer look," Indy suggested. Taking flashlights, but keeping them turned off, the campers walked beside the quarry wall. Suddenly they heard the faint rattle of gravel on the slope. It became louder as it tumbled down the cliff. Then in the glow of the green fire, the dead pine tree tilted over.

"It's going to fall!" Holly shouted.

"Here it comes!" Pete called out. "Everybody run!"

CHAPTER 15

A Scary Night

DROPPING end over end, the pine banged against the cliff in its plunge to the quarry below. As the children and Indy raced out of the way, the tree struck the ground behind them, sending up a shower of dust and broken twigs.

"Yikes!" Ricky said, glancing up. "I wonder what made it fall?"

"The question is," Indy said, "why did it fall now?"

Pam guessed that someone was trying to frighten them away, but Pete replied, "It'll take more than a green fire and a falling tree to scare us out of Castle Rock Quarry."

By flashlight they found their way back to camp. Domingo was still tied to a stake where they had left him earlier, and Pam gave the pet a hug around the neck. They kept watch in the dark for another hour. When nothing more happened Indy and his young charges settled down in their sleeping bags.

Holly and Pam lay quietly, but their eyes were wide open and their brains raced with thoughts about the mysterious quarry.

"Are you asleep, Holly?" Pam asked softly in the darkness.

"No," came the whispered reply. "Are you scared, Pam?"

"Not really," the older girl replied, "but the noises in the quarry are strange and magnified at night." She added quickly, "Let's play a game. That'll make us go to sleep."

"What kind of game?"

"Why don't we guess what all the funny noises are," Pam suggested.

Both girls quietly listened as a low moaning sound sifted down into the quarry.

"What's that?" Holly asked.

"The wind."

"Right. I guessed it too."

Next, little cheeping sounds could be heard in the distance and Holly whispered, "Tree frogs." Then came a light splash which both girls guessed at once came from a fish jumping in the pond.

Holly put her head back on the pillow and her eyes closed halfway. A tiny trickling sound came to her ears, but she was too sleepy to guess, and fell asleep. Pam, too, drifted off into dreamland.

In the tent next to the girls, Pete was still awake. The weird quarry noises kept him thinking about the strange happenings there. For a long time he puzzled over them. Suddenly he heard another sound in the distance. *Thump, thump, thump.*

"Crickets!" Pete said to himself. "What's that?"

The boy crawled out of his sleeping bag and poked his head through the tent flap. *Thump, thump, thump.*

The old pump! he thought. It's working! But Raff had said it was broken! Who could be operating it, especially in the middle of the night?

Indy was snoring lightly, so Pete did not disturb him. Instead he quietly roused Ricky. "Listen to that sound," he whispered into his brother's ear. "Come with me."

Silently, Ricky wriggled out of his bag and together the two boys made their way in darkness toward the pond. A silver slice of moon shone down into the quarry. Although it provided only dim light, it was enough for the boys to skirt around boulders in their path.

When they neared the edge of the water Pete whispered, "It is the old pump, all right." But suddenly as they drew closer, the motor stopped. All was quiet. Nothing moved.

"Maybe it wasn't the pump at all," Ricky whispered.

"We'll find out," Pete replied as he cautiously started forward again.

When the boys reached the fallen tree they climbed over it and made their way along the narrow bank between Castle Rock and the pond. In the moonlight they saw small ripples on the water.

"There's the pump," Pete said and advanced to-

135

ward it. He put his hand on the metal. *It was warm.*

"What'd I tell you!" Pete said.

"But why would anybody be trying to pump water out of the pond now?"

"Someone's trying to scare us, Ricky—the same as when they toppled the tree."

The redhead stood up to his full height and threw out his chest. "They're not scaring me," he said bravely, but suddenly he grasped Pete's arm tightly, and his teeth chattered in fright.

Ricky could only point to the surface of the pond, which had been calm a few moments before.

Twenty feet from shore the water frothed and churned. A round black form emerged for a few inches and then disappeared silently into the depths.

"Yi-yikes! The—the—monster!"

Just then another voice echoed across the quarry. "Pete! Ricky! Where are you!

"Over here, Indy," Pete shouted.

In the distance a flashlight bobbed up and down as Indy Roades hastened toward the two boys.

"We saw the monster! We really did!" Ricky called out as their Indian friend drew closer. The man shone the light on Pete and asked if he too had seen it.

"Yes, I did, Indy. Something's in that pond— a giant water snake or some kind of queer fish."

The three made their way back to the tents

"They're not scaring me," Ricky said.

where by now the girls had been awakened. Pam and Holly listened to the boys' story in awe.

"The monster might eat us!" Holly said. "I'm scared."

Indy agreed that their experience had been frightening and suggested that they pack up and ride back to Shoreham. "This is a job for the police," he said. "They can start an investigation."

"I want to stay here and solve the mystery," Pete said calmly. "We'll be safe with you, Indy."

"I'm with Pete," Pam voted without hesitation.

"Me too," Holly chimed. "I'm a lady detective."

Suddenly Ricky's worried face split into a wide grin, which looked even wider in the flashlight beam playing over him. "I'll stay too," he said. "I guess I wasn't so brave 'cause I'm hungry."

Pam chuckled. "How about some of that chocolate cake which Mother made for us to eat tomorrow?"

Indy stole a look at his wrist watch and announced that it was tomorrow already. With that, Pam removed the three-layer chocolate cake from the box in which her mother had packed it. After each of the children had eaten a plump, moist wedge of the delicious cake, Holly said, "Poor Domingo must be hungry, too."

"Here, take him a piece of cake," Pam said, and put a slice in Holly's hands.

The girl picked her way through the darkness to the place where the burro had been tethered.

"Domingo, where are you?" Holly said, looking about in the dim moonlight.

The donkey had vanished.

"Hurry everybody!" Holly cried. "Domingo's gone!"

The others came running, and Indy shone his light on the ground, where he had driven in the wooden stake to which the donkey had been tied. It was still there.

"Domingo didn't escape by himself," Indy said. "He was untied."

"Oh dear," Pam said. "There are prowlers around here. What'll we do?"

"I'd say chase them," Pete said indignantly.

Indy agreed with the suggestion. "We have to settle this sooner or later, and it might as well be now!"

With all five flashlights playing over the ground, Indy bent low to follow the tracks which the burro had made.

"They're heading right out of the quarry," Pete observed.

"That's strange," said Pam. "If the prowlers are trying to annoy us, why wouldn't they remain here?"

"I'm surprised that Domingo didn't "ee-aw" to warn us that he was being stolen," Ricky said as they neared the gap which led from the quarry.

"Whoever took Domingo went in a beeline," Indy said, "and judging from the hoofprints, the burro was going pretty fast."

"Hush!" Pam said suddenly. "I hear something."

The pursuers stopped to listen. In the distance voices could be heard.

"Come on, you stupid animal!"

"Don't stop now. Giddap!"

Pete whispered, "The thieves. We'll catch them, Indy."

Walking on tiptoes and crouching, Indy led the Hollisters behind bushes and rocks to avoid being seen. Then all at once he said, "Look there!"

Ahead of them in the semidarkness was the faint outline of a donkey. Two persons were on his back. One of them slid to the ground. The other followed.

"Shall we pounce on them?" Pete whispered.

"Now!" Indy replied.

With shrieks and war whoops the Hollisters dashed toward Domingo. For an instant, the donkey's captors stood stock still in surprise, then raced off into the night.

Reaching their pet, Pam and Holly flung themselves on Domingo. "You poor little burro," Pam said soothingly.

"We won't let those bad men take you away," Holly said, stroking the donkey's ears.

With that, Domingo lifted his head and brayed so loudly that the "ee-aw" echoed through the still night.

Pete, Ricky and Indy did not stop, however. Their flashlight beams stabbed this way and that like giant fireflies pursuing the fugitives. Finally

Indy stopped and motioned Pete and Ricky to his side. "See that big boulder?" he said. "Those fellows are hiding behind it. They're probably winded and scared."

"Yikes!" Ricky said. "If we catch them now the quarry mystery is solved!"

Indy cupped his hands and called out, "Whoever you are, come out!"

A rustling noise came from behind the boulder and two figures stepped forward. Pete shone his light in their faces, and gasped.

They were Joey Brill and Will Wilson!

CHAPTER 16

A Queer Echo

FRIGHTENED and trembling, Joey and Will stood unhappily in the glare of the flashlights. "Let us go," Joey quavered. "We want to go home!"

"I suppose that's why you took Domingo," Pam said. "You should be ashamed!"

Will spoke up. "That's exactly why we took Domingo—to get out of this place, fast!"

When asked to explain, Joey and Will said that they had overheard Dave Mead tell about the Hollisters' camping trip.

"We decided to come, too," Joey said lamely.

"To bother us, I suppose," Ricky said, as the Hollisters gathered around the embarrassed bullies.

"We wanted to drop our—your—parachute off the cliff," Will confessed. He added that his father had driven the boys to Castle Rock Quarry early that evening and they had pitched their pup tents nearby.

"We crept up to watch what you were doing," Joey went on, "and came upon Ricky and Pete walking toward the pond."

"And then we saw it!" Will said with a shudder.

"Ugh! That thing in the water!" Joey exclaimed.

"We couldn't get out of there fast enough so we borrowed Domingo. We didn't mean to steal him, honest."

"You didn't push the tree over, or start the old pump?" Pam queried.

Joey and Will denied doing this. "All we want to do is go home," Joey said. "This place is too spooky."

"Okay," Pete said. "Where is your camp?"

Joey and Will led them on a short distance to where their small tents were pitched beneath an oak tree. "I guess they were telling the truth," Pam said aside to Pete.

"You won't let the monster get us, will you, Indy?" Will pleaded.

"You'll be safe here," the Indian assured them.

"Then we'll stay until morning," Joey said in relief, "and hitch a ride back to Shoreham."

They all said good-by and on the way back to their own camp with Domingo, Pam chuckled. "If you think we were scared, what about Joey and Will."

"Those snoopers were petrified," Pete said.

The four youngsters were awakened next morning by the delightful aroma of bacon frying over an open fire.

"Breakfast is served," Indy said. "Come and get it!" The menu included scrambled eggs, bacon and bread toasted over the open fire. Pam served milk from the cooler. After the paper plates had been burned, the boys and Indy put out the fire.

"Before we go prospecting," Pete said, "I think we ought to investigate the green fire and the tree."

"We'll take a sack with us," Pam said, "just in case we see anything that looks like titanium."

After tying Domingo at camp, the children and Indy hurried to the fallen pine. While Ricky, Holly and Indy examined the dead tree, Pete and Pam climbed over it and hastened up the steep path to the top of the quarry.

In a few minutes they spotted the remains of the fire and carefully picked over the charred pieces of wood.

"Look," Pete remarked. "There's a white powder spilled here. Maybe that's what made the fire green."

The boy took the burned end of a stick with white dust on it and wrapped it in his handkerchief. Then he and Pam made their way to the spot where the pine tree had stood.

A large chunk had come out of the cliff when the tree fell. The children examined the ground around the spot, but found no footprints.

"Of course, it could have been an accident," Pete said doubtfully. "The tree was on the very edge, anyway."

But when he and Pam joined the others at the foot of the cliff, Indy said, "That pine was pushed down. Look at this." He showed them fresh marks of a crowbar at the base of the trunk.

"And someone used a chemical to make that spooky green fire," Pete reported, and showed his clue.

"Maybe Ralston or Raff are behind all this," Ricky guessed. "They don't seem too friendly."

"They might be looking for titanium, too," Pete said, "and not want us to find it."

Pam was not sure of this deduction. "It isn't fair to accuse them," she said. "We have no proof. Let's continue our prospecting. We may find clues to all our mysteries along the way."

Ricky tugged the battered felt hat down lower over his eyes and announced that he was ready.

Pete stood with hands on hips, surveying the buff-colored cliffs, and suggested that they walk to the far end of the quarry where the old crushing mill stood. That area, he could see, was dry and pebbly. First, however, the prospectors stopped at their camp to pick up Domingo, rope and tools.

Before they left, Ricky stuffed a wad of fishing line into his pocket, just in case they should circle the quarry and stop at the pond again. "I might even catch the monster," the boy thought. "But I kind of hope not."

With Pete in the lead, the party set out. Soon they crossed a small strip of dark, soggy ground, which Pam guessed was watered by an underground spring.

As the sun rose higher, the quarry rim showed clear and distinct against the blue sky. Holly happened to glance up at Castle Rock and was surprised to see Ralston watching them.

"Hi," she called cheerfully, waving her arms. The man shouted and waved back, then turned and walked along the lip of the cliff, looking down at the ground as if trying to locate something.

"He seems friendly enough today," Pete said. "Perhaps you're right, Pam. He could be innocent."

While Ricky continued to circle around the quarry like a bird dog, Pete moved straight ahead, leading Domingo. The sack on the burro's back became heavier and heavier as the children put stones into it. As Pete was about to pick up another specimen, he knelt down and motioned the others back.

"Crickets!" he called out. "Footprints. Lots of them. Look at these, Indy!"

The Indian and the young prospectors came forward carefully, so as not to disturb the signs which Pete had discovered. It looked as if something had been dragged over the dusty ground, and the spot seemed well trampled.

"It's nowhere near the pond or boats," Pam said. "I wonder what people were doing over here?"

"They might be visitors just like us," Holly said. "Maybe they were playing games."

Pete was so interested in the tracks that he gave up rock hunting for a while and pressed forward to see where they led. One set of footprints went to the quarry wall where they disappeared into a pile of dry brush.

"That's funny," the boy thought, and called to the others to hurry.

"What do you make of this, Indy?" Pete said. The Indian snapped off a piece of the brush and glanced at the top of the cliff. "It might have fallen down sometime before," he said, "but on the other hand, it could be camouflage."

"Let's move it," Ricky suggested.

With everyone pulling and hauling, the dry brush was moved aside, revealing a small cleft in the rocks.

"This looks like a passage!" Indy said.

"But it's hardly wide enough to get through," Pete remarked.

"If I take a deep breath I think I can slip by," Ricky said.

Indy Roades took his flashlight from the supply bag on Domingo, and, one at a time, the prospectors squeezed through the split in the rock. Domingo looked disappointed that he could not go, but stood quietly beside the brush.

With Ricky in the lead, the adventurers pressed forward. Suddenly the passage widened into a room.

"Oh look!" Ricky cried out as Indy played his light around the place. "This looks like a—a weather bureau!"

Along one wall were rows of wind charts, and below them a carton of instruments. There were

"This looks like a passage!"

also strings of colored lights, a stack of parachutes, a pile of flat balloons and several tanks of gas to inflate them.

"Crickets!" Pete cried out. "This must be where Mr. Link works on his invention."

"But where is he now?" Holly wondered.

"And why doesn't he pick up his mail?" Pete asked.

"Both Mr. Kinder and Mr. Link are connected with this quarry," Pam said, worried, "and both of them have disappeared."

Now Indy looked uneasily about the rock room and the children shivered a little.

"Maybe the monster got them," Ricky whispered.

Pam reminded them that Mr. Anthony had said that his friend lived where he was working on the invention. "So Mr. Link must have his sleeping quarters in another cave," the girl reasoned.

Being careful not to disturb the cache they had found, the explorers returned single file to where Domingo waited patiently.

"Let's make search teams," Pete suggested. "I think it is more important to find Mr. Link than to go on prospecting. He may need help."

Indy agreed. "We'll look around for an hour. Then we can meet at camp to decide what to do next."

Ricky and Holly volunteered to climb up to Castle Rock and look around there. From that height they might be able to spot another cave. "But be careful," Pam warned them.

She and Pete set off in another direction with Domingo, while Indy decided to search on the far side of the quarry behind the crushing mill.

Holding hands, the two younger children scrambled up the steep, gravelly path. After reaching the top, they entered the round turret and looked out of the rock window. They scanned the cliffs for a while, but no strangers were in sight—not even Ralston.

Ricky turned and his eyes lighted on a big stone, which Sue had used for her throne on the day of the picnic. Again he had an urge to move it. This time he had a helper equally as curious as he was.

"I think that rock is sitting in a hole or something," the redhead declared. "Come on, give me a hand."

Although the children tugged and hauled at the stone, it did not move. But Ricky would not give up easily. After running back into the woods, he returned with a strong, slender stick, and pried one end of it under the rock.

"Look, Holly," he said jubilantly, "it's moving."

The heavy rock moved far enough for the children to get their fingers under it for a better grip. They tugged again and the stone rolled to one side.

Beneath it was a hole large enough for a person to squeeze through. It led deep down into the ground.

"A tunnel!" Ricky exclaimed. "Yikes, I like tunnels, 'cause they make echoes." He lay flat on the ground and called down into the black well. There was no echo immediately, but a few seconds later a muffled sound came to his ears.

"What a funny kind of an echo," Holly remarked. "I never heard one like that before. Let me have a turn."

She shouted down into the hole and listened. Silence. Then an odd wailing sound came faintly to their ears.

Ricky scratched his head and wrinkled his nose. "That must be a long, long way down." He snapped his fingers. "Yikes, maybe it leads to an underground river full of fish."

"You're silly," said Holly. "It's so dark the fish couldn't see where to swim."

But Ricky would not be dissuaded. From his pocket he pulled the long ball of fishing line. On one end of the string was a small sinker and a hook stuck into a piece of cork. Ricky removed the cork and let the line pay out far down into the hole.

Holly's eyes opened wide with amazement as she watched the fishing line go even deeper. Ricky jiggled it, and felt the lead weight bang back and forth on the walls of the deep shaft.

Finally the sinker reached the bottom. Ricky jiggled the line and said, "Come on, fish, bite on the hook."

"But there isn't even a worm on it," Holly said, with a giggle.

Suddenly Ricky gave a startled gasp. "Holly!" he cried out. "Something's tugging at my line!"

CHAPTER 17

Daring Explorers

ANOTHER tug came at the line. This one was so strong that it nearly yanked the string from Ricky's hands.

"Pull it up!" Holly cried. "You've got a big fish."

The redhead dragged the line out of the hole hand over hand, but it felt light. Finally the hook appeared, but there was no lead weight on the end of the line. It was gone!

"Why would the fish take the weight and not the hook?" Ricky asked, looking perplexed.

Holly, too, thought that this was peculiar and suggested that they hurry down to tell Indy and the others about it. Ricky put the hook back into the cork and wadded the string in his pocket. With that the two children hurried out of the turret and scampered down the steep path to the bottom of the quarry.

"Indy! Pete! Pam!" the youngsters shouted, waving their arms.

"What happened? What did you find?" Pam asked eagerly as she and Pete ran up to them. Quickly Holly explained, and when Indy joined them on the run a short time later Ricky poured out the story.

"Perhaps the lead weight was snagged in the deep pit and pulled off," Indy said.

"Something tugged at it," Ricky insisted. "Honest! Come with us and we'll show you." The two hurried on ahead and the rest followed, with Pete leading Domingo by the halter.

After plodding to the top of Castle Rock again, the searchers stared at the hole which the youngsters had uncovered.

"Somebody must have known about this," Pete said. "Or else they wouldn't have covered it with the rock."

Indy thought that this might have been done for protection to keep picnickers from falling down the deep natural well.

"Let me show you how it echoes," Ricky said. He leaned down and called his name into the black hole. The boy smiled and waited for the echo. But none came. Then Holly tried, with the same disappointing results.

"We did hear an echo before," Holly said.

As the two younger children kept calling down into the pit, Pete beckoned Pam to one side. "I think somebody is really down there, Pam." He reminded his sister that Sid Raff had appeared and vanished quickly near the old pump. Perhaps, Pete reasoned, the man had found a hidden cleft like the one leading into Link's balloon cave.

"You mean this well might connect with a cave like that?" Pam asked, raising her eyebrows.

"It could be," said Pete. "Listen, Pam, I have a plan." Then in a loud voice Pete went on:

"Indy, I'd like to go down into that hole with Pam. We think it may lead into a hidden cave. And who knows? Mr. Link may be there. Do we have a strong rope?"

"Underneath the seat in the truck," Indy replied. "But this idea of yours is dangerous. I don't think I should let you do it."

"I'll be careful," Pete promised, as Ricky dashed off to fetch the rope.

Pete suggested that Indy could tie one end of the rope to him, and the other end to the burro. "With Domingo's help I would be easy to pull up in case I got stuck."

"I want to follow you down," Pam declared.

When Ricky returned with the rope, he and Holly clamored for the same kind of adventure, but their brother said, "I have a more important job for you to do." The younger children were to return to the quarry floor and examine the brush-grown wall near the old pump.

"See if you can find a hidden crevice in the rock," Pete told them. "And if you do find an opening, call into it just as loudly as you can. If Pam and I are down in there somewhere we might be able to hear you and find your entrance."

Eagerly Ricky and Holly started down the trail.

When they had gone Indy protested that he wanted to be the one to explore the Castle Rock tunnel.

"If anything happens you can come after us," Pete said. Then he pointed out that he and Pam were smaller and might make the descent more easily.

Finally the Indian consented. As he tied one end of the rope securely around Pete's chest, the boy fastened his flashlight to his belt. Then they discussed signals which they might send along the rope by tugging it.

One tug would mean "Send Pam down." Two tugs would mean "I'll explore." Three tugs would be a signal to pull up.

After he had tied the other end of the rope around Domingo, Indy let Pete down into the hole and paid out the rope hand over hand, the muscles of his strong arms bulging.

"Take care," Indy said, as Pete's head disappeared.

Finally the taut rope slackened. "Pete must have reached the bottom," Pam said and put her ear to the hole. From below she could hear muffled sounds which sounded like Pete's voice but she could not be certain.

Suddenly the rope was tugged once. "Send Pam," it meant. Indy hauled up the slack line and tied it around Pam, who also took a flashlight. She was lowered into the hole the same way. When the girl had reached the bottom Indy felt two tugs on the

"Take care," Indy said.

rope. So they were going to explore! The Indian silently wished them luck and safety.

Meanwhile, far below, Pete and Pam flashed their lights about a rock tunnel in which they found themselves.

"This is a natural cave formation," Pete said and started along a dank stone corridor.

"I wonder where it leads," Pam asked, and her voice bounced back and forth between the cold, wet walls.

As they pressed slowly forward Pete made a mental picture of the gloomy tunnel so they could find their way back. Everything was quiet except for water trickling down the face of the rock. Ricky and Holly could not be heard. Perhaps, Pete thought, the younger children could not find an outside entrance.

"Look!" Pam said as her light suddenly shone into a small crevice on the right side of the tunnel. "I could squeeze through it," she said and beamed her light into the narrow bypath.

Pete suggested that they carry on straight ahead. His suggestion was rewarded, for ten feet farther on the ceiling sloped low and they turned a sharp corner.

From the darkness ahead somebody cried out, "Who's there?"

Another voice called faintly, "We're saved!"

With hearts pounding, Pete and Pam suddenly found themselves in a cave which appeared to be sealed off by a jumble of rocks. At the far end sat two men, shielding their eyes from the bright rays of the flashlights.

"Mr. Kinder!" Pete cried out.

"Is that you, Mr. Kinder?" Pam asked.

The man, who had a heavy growth of whiskers, replied, "Yes, it is I, but we can't see. Your light is blinding us."

Pete and Pam put handkerchiefs over the lenses of their flashlights, producing a dim glow in the stone chamber. Then they hastened over to the two men.

"This is Mr. Elmer Link," Mr. Kinder said and introduced the Hollisters to a thin little man with a large gray mustache.

"The amateur weatherman!" Pete cried out. "Why are you imprisoned here?"

"A rock slide covered the entrance," Mr. Link said in a thin wheezy voice. The weatherman explained that he and Mr. Kinder were old friends and both had known about the quarry's peculiar caves for many years.

"So when I wanted to do some secret experiments," Mr. Link said, "I came here to be alone. At night I sent up my balloons from the center of the quarry. My workshop is in another cave but this is where I lived."

The children saw that it was well stocked with canned goods and bottles of soda and furnished with a cot and table.

"I came here to visit Elmer the day you called on me," Mr. Kinder told the children. "That night the landslide trapped us."

"Was it you who called down?" Mr. Link asked.

Pete explained about Ricky and Holly and their "echo."

"We were examining the hole when we heard the children call," Mr. Kinder explained. "I shouted back as loud as I could. Just then my flashlight went dead so I went back to fetch Elmer's."

"And I continued to call," Mr. Link said in his frail voice, "but I guess I wasn't loud enough."

"The tunnel bends," Pete said. "It muffles sound, I think."

"Even Pete's strong voice was hard to hear," Pam told them.

"Anyway, when I heard something coming down hitting the side of the tunnel, I grabbed at it and got the fishing weight."

"When I returned, I called and called," Mr. Kinder said, "but I guess you children were gone."

"We came back in here, hoping and waiting for rescue," Mr. Link concluded.

The two children led the men back along the tunnel and when they came to the dangling rope Pete tied it first on the old rock hound. Then he gave three tugs.

The man's feet left the ground and up, up he went into the dark shaft until he reached the top.

Now the children could hear Indy's exclamation of amazement.

"He expected to see me," Pam said with a chuckle. "And instead there was a whiskery man!"

When the rope was lowered again Pete fastened Mr. Link securely to it. After three tugs the slender inventor was hauled to the top of Castle Rock.

Pam was about to make her ascent when suddenly the two of them heard cries which sounded far, far off.

"Holly and Ricky!" Pete said. "They must have found a way into this place." After Pete gave the "explore" signal again, he and Pam retraced their way along the tunnel. The sound seemed to come from the cleft which Pam had seen earlier.

"Holly! Ricky! Here we are! Wait for us!" Pete cried.

The sister and brother wriggled through the tight passage which suddenly opened into a tall, craggy cavern, with pale shafts of light slanting down from above.

Pete and Pam kept calling, and the response from Holly and Ricky grew louder with each step. "Look, there they are!" Pete exclaimed as the younger children burst through a thin crevice in the opposite wall.

"I thought there might be a way out!" Pete said.

"We found it all right," Ricky announced proudly. "It was a little tiny hole which we had to crawl through on hands and knees."

Holly's eyes roamed around the vaultlike cavern. "This is awful spooky," she said. "Come on, Pam, let's go back and tell the others."

As they started toward the exit which led to the quarry cliff, the youngsters suddenly heard a splash behind them. They whirled and Pete stabbed his flashlight through the semidarkness. The rays shone off a small pool of water the size of a barrel top in the middle of the rock floor.

Suddenly a strange, goggled head rose out of the water and a dripping black figure hauled itself from the pool and stood facing them.

CHAPTER 18

Good for Bad

WHEN the black-clad figure advanced a few steps toward the four Hollisters, Holly cried out, "Oh, it's the mon—"

"No, it isn't!" Pete said angrily. "It's a man in a skin-diving suit. And he's through scaring us. Oh, Indy Roades! Here's the man we've been looking for!"

Upon hearing this the skin diver turned, flopped across the stone cave with his flippers, and jumped into the pool, disappearing beneath the black water.

"Oh Pete!" Pam exclaimed. "Your trick saved us!"

"Now we have to capture him!" her brother replied. He turned to Ricky and Holly. "Show us the way you got in here. I have a hunch that fellow will appear in the quarry pond before long."

Ricky led the way into the crevice and through a narrow, jagged passage with the others close behind him. After wriggling along for a few minutes, they saw daylight and crawled out through a low opening in the cliff wall. They worked their way

around a heavy screen of brush and found themselves close to the old pump.

No sooner had they accustomed their eyes to the
sunlight when they saw ripples forming in the middle of the pond. Then the same black-helmeted
head came to the surface and the skin diver swam
quickly to the edge of the water below Castle Rock.

"Pam! Holly! Call for help!" Pete ordered. "Get
Indy! Ricky and I'll try to stop the skin diver!"

While the girls backed off from the cliff and
shrieked for Indy, the boys ran toward the spot
where the black rubber-clad figure had climbed out
of the pond. The man dropped his oxygen tank
and ripped the mask from his head.

"It's Ralston!" Pete shouted. "He's the mystery
man who's been trying to scare us."

The diver ran awkwardly along the narrow strip
of ground between Castle Rock and the pond.
Finding himself blocked by the fallen tree, he
turned and started back. But his escape was cut off
at the other end of the narrow stretch by the two
Hollister boys.

Hearing shouts, Pete and Ricky turned to see
Indy, followed by Mr. Kinder and his friend Link
running down the steep path into the quarry.

At the sight of reinforcements Ralston stopped.
With a quick glance up at the Castle Rock, he
kicked off his flippers. As Pete and Ricky darted forward to seize him, he sprang out of reach and began to scale the steep rock wall.

"He's pretty desperate to get away," Pete said as the brothers stood at the base of the cliff and looked up at the ungainly figure clutching at the small outcroppings of rock.

"He'll never make it," Ricky predicted.

With a sudden scream the climber lost his footing, flung himself away from the quarry wall, and flew over the boys' heads. With a great splash he landed in the pond on his back.

But instead of swimming toward the shore again, the skin diver lay still for a moment, then began to sink beneath the surface.

"He's knocked out," Pete cried. Speedily, he and Ricky kicked off their shoes and without a moment's hesitation dived in after the stricken Ralston. They pulled him ashore just as the three men, Pam and Holly arrived on the scene.

Indy helped to skin the man out of his rubber diving suit. After Pam had chafed his wrists, Ralston opened his eyes.

"You have some questions to answer," Mr. Kinder said sternly. "What have you been up to in my quarry?"

"And is Sid Raff in on this?" Pam asked.

"Where is he now?" Pete asked the half-dazed man. "Is he in one of the caves, too?"

Ralston shook his head no and pointed feebly cross the quarry, where a small puff of dust arose from the old crushing plant.

"He's hiding in there, men!" Ricky declared. "Come on! Let's catch him, too!"

Leaving the two girls with Mr. Link and Mr. Kinder to guard the prisoner, Indy, Ricky and Pete raced across the quarry. They arrived at the door of the old building just in time to see Sid Raff hastening out with a large carton. As Indy Roades grabbed him tightly, the man dropped the box, spilling its contents of stones on the ground.

"We've got your friend Ralston and we want you too!" the Indian said with authority. "You're going to tell us what all this monkey business has been about!"

"It's not my fault. I didn't do anything," Sid Raff protested.

"This carton was full of titanium," Ricky exclaimed, picking up some gold-threaded stones.

"You told us there was none around," Pete accused the man.

"Ralston didn't want anybody to know about it," Raff replied. "You were getting too nosey. That's why he told me to get these samples out of the quarry. It was all his idea," he added as the boys and Indy led him back to the others.

Coming face to face, the two prisoners glowered at each other for a moment.

"You weren't going to get caught, were you?" Raff said sarcastically.

"It's your fault," Ralston snapped back. "You

promised to keep these kids away so we could do our prospecting without being seen."

"Silence!" Mr. Kinder demanded. "I own this quarry and have a right to know what you have been up to."

Ralston heaved a long sigh and said, "All right. I'll tell you the truth. I was looking for titanium and I think I'd have found it if these Hollisters hadn't come along."

Ralston said that after studying geological maps he had decided that a titanium vein could be located in or near the quarry. "I got this skin-diving equipment to study the quarry walls deep below the surface of the pond," he said. Pointing to the carton of stones which Ricky had picked up and brought along, he added, "I found that titanium on the bottom of the pond."

"And tried to frighten us away," Pam declared, "by making us think that you were a monster."

"Well, it didn't work!" Ricky said. "'Cause we're not afraid of monsters!"

Ralston managed a wry smile and said that Pam had nearly knocked the wind out of him when the girl accidently fell in the pond while chasing the parachute.

Mr. Kinder surprised everyone by saying that he knew all about the secret caves and underground waterway into the pond, but he had no idea that anyone besides Mr. Link knew anything about them.

"You weren't so smart," Ralston said testily. "I discovered the waterway passage while exploring the pond. I let Raff in on the scheme so that he could help me find the titanium vein and keep visitors away."

"But I didn't harm anybody," Sid Raff pleaded. "Even when Mr. Link would send up his weather balloons at night, I didn't bother him."

"How good of you," remarked the little inventor. "You saw Kinder and me go into my cave just before the landslide, yet you made no attempt to rescue us."

"We knew there was food enough for weeks," Ralston said. "This was a chance to get Kinder and you out of the way long enough for us to find the titanium vein. I was sure we were close to it."

"Then we'd have got you out," Raff assured them.

"After the quarry was mine," Ralston told them, "I'd have sold it to a big company for a good price."

Mr. Kinder's eyes flashed and he looked straight at Ralston. "Were you the one who was trying to buy my quarry cheap?" he asked.

The geologist admitted shamefacedly that it was he, acting through an intermediary.

"You meanie!" Pam exclaimed. "Trying to buy this valuable property so cheaply."

"And to think I almost sold it," Mr. Kinder said.

"The Hollisters saved you from that," Indy said proudly.

Ralston looked at the ground glumly and Raff said, "I wish I'd never got into this."

"Eee-aw! Eee-aw!" Domingo brayed from the top of Castle Rock.

"Oh dear!" Pam said. "He wants to join the excitement! Is he tied up there, Indy?"

When the Indian nodded yes, the sisters hastened to retrieve their burro friend. As the girls climbed up the path, Ricky and Pete continued to question the two men.

Ralston, they learned, had taken the car keys the day of the picnic, and had written the threatening note. He also had started the old pump to frighten the campers. It was he, too, who had built the fire on the rim of the quarry and added a chemical powder to make it burn green.

"You made the tree fall too, I suppose," Pete declared. "You could have hurt us."

"I only meant to frighten you," Ralston insisted.

"In all the years I've been rock hunting in this quarry," Mr. Kinder mused, "I never found titanium. No wonder," he added. "It's all in the pond."

"Not all of it," Pete said, remembering the small piece Ricky had found. He took it from his pocket.

Mr. Kinder put on his spectacles and studied the stone. "One little piece doesn't make a vein," he said. "Where did you find this?"

"Up on the path," Ricky replied, pointing.

Pam and Holly, meanwhile, had reached the top of Castle Rock, untied Domingo, and started back down again. As they passed the place where Pam had loosened the rock earlier, Holly climbed out gingerly onto the jumbled landslide and gathered the big stone in her arms. This she put in a sack on Domingo's back and continued down until they reached the edge of the pond.

"Here's another rock, prospector Ricky," Holly said as she dumped the whitish piece at his feet.

Upon seeing the underside of the stone, Ralston's eyes opened wide and he said, "That's—"

"Titanium!" Pete cried out.

Mr. Kinder adjusted his glasses and looked at it closer. "By thunder it is!" he said. "And a real chunk! Where'd you find it, Holly?"

"In the same place where Ricky found his piece," she replied.

Mr. Kinder was so excited that he hopped onto Domingo and urged the burro quickly to the spot. The others ran along behind him, with the exception of Ralston and Raff, whom Indy guarded closely. The agile old rock hound scrambled out on the landslide and poked among the rocks.

"It's here! It is a vein of titanium!" he cried out. Then he grabbed Mr. Link and the two old cronies danced a jig.

Ricky and Holly giggled, and danced around too.

"What a happy day for us!" Pam cried out in

"Where did you find it, Holly?"

delight. "Mr. Kinder, you found your titanium, and—oh, Mr. Link, we forgot to tell you—the weather bureau wants to buy your talking paracute!"

"Really? How do you know that?"

Pam quickly told him about their visit to New York. When she had finished by giving him Hootnanny's name and address, the thin little man was quiet a moment. Then he said quietly, "You young detectives have made two old men very happy today."

On the way back to the pond, Pete asked, "What are you going to do with Raff and Ralston?"

Mr. Kinder pondered the question before replying. "Their plan to cheat me failed," he said finally. "All they really did was trespass and try to frighten people. Perhaps they've learned their lesson."

Facing the two crestfallen villains he said, "I could have you arrested for the trouble you've caused," he said, "but instead I'm going to banish you forever from Castle Rock Quarry. Now go, and don't come back again!"

Sid Raff asked permission to re-enter the cave and bring out some clothes for his friend Ralston. When he had done this, the two men walked dejectedly from the quarry, and as far as the Hollisters know they never returned again.

As the pair trudged out, they passed the Hollister station wagon coming along the bumpy road at the entrance to the Castle Rock property. Mrs.

Hollister was at the wheel. Beside her sat Sue and Daffy. The dark-haired girl held Maddie-Poo in her arms.

When they drove up to the camp the young prospectors raced to meet them. Mrs. Hollister stopped the car and called out the window, "I brought some more soda pop and another chocolate cake for you."

"Oh good, Mother!" Pam cried, as the children gathered around the car. "We can have a big celebration right now!"

"We caught the monster and found Mr. Kinder and Mr. Link and titanium and we're starving for lunch," Ricky reported all in one breath.

"How exciting!" Daffy said. "Oh, I wish I might have seen it all."

"Even though you weren't with us," Pam remarked, "you did a lot to help solve the mysteries."

Mrs. Hollister laughed. "Then your camping trip was a success!"

"It certainly was," declared Mr. Kinder, as he, Mr. Link and Indy joined the party. Domingo trotted in last.

Sue climbed out of the car holding her doll proudly. "Look!" she announced happily to one and all. "Maddie-Poo's head is on straight and she's all better—and, and Joey's mother spanked him!"

Then the little girl turned her eyes toward the quarry pond. "Has the bad old monster gone?"

she asked. "'Cause I don't want him to eat up Maddie-Poo."

Everyone laughed, and Pete said, "The monster has gone from Castle Rock Quarry forever!"

"Which means I'm going to have some fun," Ricky declared. He ran to the boys' tent, popped in, and popped out holding his parachute.

"I'll beat anybody to the top of Castle Rock!" he challenged.

"Not me!" Daffy retorted, and dust flew as the youngsters raced off side by side.